Getaway

Also by Glen Pourciau

View
Invite

GETAWAY

Glen Pourciau

Four Way Books

Tribeca

Library of Congress Cataloging-in-Publication Data

Names: Pourciau, Glen, 1951- author.
Title: Getaway / by Glen Pourciau.
Description: 1st. | New York : Four Way Books, [2021] |
Identifiers: LCCN 2021005287 | ISBN 9781945588976 (paperback)
Classification: LCC PS3616.O868 G48 2021 | DDC 813/.6--dc23
LC record available at https://lccn.loc.gov/2021005287

This book is manufactured in the United States of America and printed on
acid-free paper.

Four Way Books is a not-for-profit literary press. We are grateful for the assistance
we receive from individual donors, public arts agencies, and private foundations.

This publication is made possible with public funds from the
New York State Council on the Arts, a state agency.

We are a proud member of the Community of Literary Magazines and Presses.

Contents

BUFFALO

I've been looking without success for more regular work, but to make ends meet I earn money by watching houses for people on vacation. This one guy whose house I've been watching is the biggest jerk I've ever worked for, the reach of his rapacious and mean-spirited nature stretching all the way across the Atlantic Ocean. Our agreement is for me to drop by his place on Wednesdays and Sundays while he travels Europe for six weeks, and he's provided me with a highly specific to-do list that shows he wants to leave as few decisions as possible to my discretion. It includes the exact number of windows I should check, all the places I should search on all fours for leaks, the number of times I should flush his toilets, which day of the week I should start his Audi, and how many minutes I should let water run from his faucets and his shower and tub. He has friends who've hired me so he must know what my rate is, but he's one of those guys who likes to grind you down to get the best deal, to exploit any angle against you.

The day we met to discuss the job he said he'd talked to one of his friends who knows where I live. My house was closer

3

to his house than Charlie's, he argued, so I'd spend less on gas working for him, which in his mind meant I shouldn't charge him the same price, though their houses were less than a mile apart. I said if I charged him less it could get back to my other customers in town, who could in turn want a reduction in their rates. He didn't care in the least about my end of it and he kept at me, saying our deal would be more long term than my usual deal. I replied that his assumption was incorrect, that I often worked for people for months at a time, and without pausing for a second he said he wanted to know whose houses I'd watched for months so he could call them to verify the facts. I stared at him, resenting his attitude, and then I said he could take my rate or leave it. I didn't tell him he didn't know what he was talking about and it was none of his business calling up my customers and asking them how long they'd left town. I needed the work and didn't want him complaining to his friends who'd hired me, but I wasn't going to let him buffalo me. One more word out of him, I muttered inside my head, and I'd be out the door. If he did complain to his friends, I'd explain that he wouldn't accept my terms and there was a personality conflict between us. But he didn't say that one more word and he agreed to the price I'd quoted him. Still, I could tell he didn't like it and never would.

I'd learned from Charlie that he worked as a negotiator for a living, and I could easily see him skinning people alive at every opportunity. He'd try to get back at me, I figured, and I resolved to be vigilant with Mr. Buffalo.

So I go about my duties after he flies off, following his detailed instructions, standing at the toilets after each flush until the water stops running and so forth, and I'm thinking as I look over his things of all the tips he's shaving from European service people. And because he's such a prick I go to his walk-in closet to catch a whiff of his smell. I find that everyone has a closet smell they leave behind in their clothes. In his case I want to identify the smell as something I don't like, something I'll notice whenever I stick my head in his closet and can curse as a somewhat intimate substitute for cursing him, which for business reasons I could never do out loud. But I go no further with the invasiveness and stick with the items on my list. I don't rummage through his desk or bedroom drawers or switch on his TV and watch adult channels through his cable service. I turn the engine over in his Audi and let it idle for six minutes as requested, let the water in his shower and tub run for two minutes, check the thermostats, blah blah blah, business as usual, until one Wednesday I see a folded sheet of paper in his mail, no envelope, dark lettering showing through the back of the page. I carry the stack of mail into his house, enter the alarm code and take the mail to his kitchen counter.

The note is unsigned and written in uneven letters with a black marker. It says that rats are congregating in the guy's backyard. The note writer says he's seen them crawling under the back fence, and he's put his foot up on the rail near sunset and peeked over the pickets and seen them skittering across the yard. As far as he can see, no traps or bait stations have been put out, though this pattern of activity has been going on for weeks. The rats are a menace to the neighborhood, he says, and action should be taken. *IT IS YOUR DUTY!* the note concludes.

I take a look out back and notice rat turds on the patio and on the stone border around the flowerbeds and snap pictures of them. I go inside and pull out my phone and then email the information about the note and the rats to Mr. Buffalo. I attach images of the rat turds. He's asked me to email him once a week with a report and I've sent him two messages before this one saying everything's in order, but he apparently hasn't had a chance to acknowledge receipt. I picture him ignoring his phone, sitting at an outdoor café enjoying wine and cheese and breathing second-hand smoke, but as I walk through his house, checking windows and making sure nothing has sprung a leak, my phone rings.

It's him, agitated and wanting to know how I plan to deal with the rats. I ask him what he wants me to do. I'm not going to set the rat agenda and have him object to it when he gets back and say he's not paying for any traps I purchase. I can sniff right away that he has no rat experience and after he admits it I offer to buy a few traps and put them around his backyard. He wants me to use humane traps and I don't have a problem with that. I ask him to agree to reimburse me for the traps and my time. I remind him we discussed that any unforeseen duties would require extra payment. He hesitates, but he's got an international-long-distance tab running and for that reason he lacks the patience to haggle. He agrees but has an attitude about it, and he abruptly hangs up on me, as if I'm to blame for putting him at a disadvantage. After he cuts me off, I talk to my phone like I'm still talking to him, speaking his part and answering myself, and I begin to think what I'll do if I catch rats alive.

At home, I decide to write down everything that's happened, trying to keep my thoughts straight, and I read over the copy and adjust it repeatedly. I shop for traps online, scanning reviews and watching video demos, and I order three wire-mesh traps designed so that a metal door closes behind the rat, leaving it trapped in the cage. If I catch some other animal, I can raise the door and release it. I forward the receipt to his email, and several days later the traps are delivered. I take them to his house and put two on the patio and the other on the edge of a flowerbed.

I consider buying more traps, but I don't know if he'll balk at paying more or if he'll pay me anything if I don't catch any rats. And it occurs to me that if I catch some rats and drive somewhere and release them, he could say I'm lying just to take his money. Should I drown them and put them in his freezer so he'll know I'm not faking. But then he could claim I trapped them somewhere else. I become furious thinking how he could twist the story to create a reason not to pay me what I'm owed, and I make up my mind that I'm not driving to his house every day to check the traps. I can't assume I'd be compensated and I don't want to have that conversation with him, even over email. So to hell with him, I'll check the traps on my regular visits.

The next day he emails me for a rat update, and I reply that I've set three traps that catch rats alive. He emails back, asking if I've had success catching any yet. I remind him it's early in the morning where I am and besides that it's not one of my scheduled days. I wait for an answer, nothing comes, and I stick with the idea that if he doesn't want to pay for more visits, I'm not going to make them. Maybe he thinks I'll go over without checking with him, but I'm not falling for that one.

Next visit, I see some fresh rat turds on the patio. The bait's been nibbled in one of the traps and I see rat turds inside its door, but the door remains open. I go in the house and send the latest images to him, and I receive his reply within minutes. He's annoyed to be worrying about rats while he's on vacation and he's wondering if I've made up the story of the rats and the anonymous note to agitate him because of our minor disagreement over my fee. I could have planted the rat turds and written the alleged anonymous note myself, he raves on as if he's convinced that's exactly what I've done and made up the story about finding the note in his mailbox. I send him a message denying his fantasies are true, and he replies again, demanding to know how he can be sure how many rats I've captured, assuming for the moment, he writes, that there are rats in his yard. Do I expect to be paid by the animal and, if so, how will I prove how many I've caught? I don't answer, not wanting to invite another reply. From the look of his backyard, he never goes out there— no grill and not a single chair on his patio. These rats could have been running around inside his back fence for months without him knowing it, and now I'm stuck dealing with them and his escalating paranoia. I decide that I'll do my job and make my weekly reports, but until he returns the subject of rats is closed.

Two more rat emails from him follow. I don't answer either of them, and a week later he sends an email threatening to get even with me if I neglect my duties or damage his house in any way. I continue with my reports without reacting to his comments, and on one occasion he sends a reply suggesting that I'm fabricating the reports and that I'm not watching his house at all. He asks me to sign and date a sheet of paper whenever I come to the house and leave the sheet on the kitchen counter. I don't tell him that I've removed the traps from his yard and stacked them on a table in his garage.

Despite ignoring his messages, inside I'm seething. Is he purposely fabricating a scenario that will allow him to argue he owes me nothing for trips to his house he'll say I never made or for trapping rats he'll say never existed? Even the log he's asked me to sign could have been made anywhere, he could claim, and then brought to his house and placed on his kitchen counter. Does he want me to fear the damage he could cause to me if he tells this story to his friends?

The week before he returns, I put the traps in the yard and place strips of raw bacon inside them. The following day I make a trip to the house to check the traps, and I see rats pacing inside two of the cages as I approach. I carry the cages in the house and set them side by side on the kitchen floor. I raise the cage doors, the rats bolt free, and I take little notice of where they run. I leave the pantry door open a crack and also open one of the cabinets under the kitchen sink. I take the traps outside and set them again, and before I leave the house I walk into his closet and curse him and his smell, picturing rats prowling his shelves and curling up in his shoes.

On my last visit I perform my duties, and though the rats don't show themselves I see tiny turds they've dropped on his floor. I laugh as I think of Mr. Buffalo coming across them and later being spooked by the sound of rats in his bedroom while, exhausted from his flight, he tries to sleep. I imagine him dreaming of rats crawling over his ear, sniffing his skin and breath, their toenails scratching at his temple, and even if he refuses to pay me a dime for watching his house these images will more than make up for it.

I can't sleep thinking of his anger when he realizes rats are in his house. He'll call me, maybe in the middle of the night, demanding an explanation, his pulse racing like rat feet in his head. Rats can squeeze in through the smallest openings, I'll tell him. You may never be able to say for sure how they got in.

FAUX BOIS

I'd walked the sidewalks and alleys of our neighborhood for years and had gotten to know some of the neighbors this way, one of them Olivia, an older woman who lived across the street and five or six houses down. I first spoke with her when she was planting clusters of periwinkles in her front beds. "They love the heat," she said. Sometime later we struck up a conversation about our vegetable gardens and she led me to her backyard to see her tomatoes and bell peppers. We then sat in a shaded area on a weathered teak bench where she commented on the faux bois birdbath in front of us. She and her late husband had found it in an antiques market during a road trip and had driven it home with them. And though our talk turned to our favorite vegetables, my eyes lingered on the birdbath, on its nuance and texture.

Olivia died of heart failure in her mid-eighties, about a year after we sat on the bench. A for-sale sign soon appeared in her yard, and I assumed that like many aging homes in our neighborhood, it would be torn down by the new owners and replaced with some imposing two-story monument to affluence. But the house remained on the market for months, and I watched the beds become overgrown and the graying wood fence around the backyard sag, several of its pickets rotting and cracking. And then one afternoon, at the end of a long walk, I noticed that the sign had at last been removed.

There was no discernible activity at the house for some time, but I began to watch it closely after twice seeing a white pickup truck parked in front of it. While walking through Olivia's alley following the second pickup sighting, I saw that her decrepit fence had been knocked down and hauled off, and in its place stood a temporary fence. The birdbath and bench remained in place, and I asked myself what would happen to them. The buyers would likely want to erase all signs of Olivia's life in the house, and I imagined they'd view the bench and birdbath as pieces to retire so they could put their own stamp on the property.

Vance and I had lived in our house for forty years, raising our two children there and building our lives together. At times I thought of our house being flattened by the next owner without the slightest regard for its history. Perhaps for that reason as much as any other I felt a desire to protect Olivia's property, and I could see only one way to act on that desire. On my walks and at home, I kept thinking of the birdbath as something that could be salvaged from the demolition and removal of what was left of her life.

So I took it as providence when I saw an empty wagon near the garbage container behind Olivia's house as I walked her alley. I'd never seen the wagon before, but I guessed that the future residents had come across it and had put it out to be taken away by the city. I pondered the wagon for at least a minute while making up my mind, my pulse going wild as I picked up its handle and opened the gate. I pulled it toward the birdbath, alert for sound and movement in the yard. I worked the birdbath off its base and lifted the base into the wagon, telling myself not to appear rushed or to look around to see if anyone was watching. I rolled the wagon through the open gate, no one else that I caught sight of in the alley and no one coming near me on the way home. I hid the base between our fence and the back of our garage and then drove our SUV to the alley to pick up the rest of the birdbath. I had just enough strength to heave it over the bumper.

The whole thing went off without any problem that I was aware of, though someone could have been watching me from a window. I didn't tell Vance, unsure how to justify myself to him. I had a sense of accomplishment that I'd saved the birdbath and wagon and they were now mine, but in the heat of the transfer I hadn't considered what I'd do with the birdbath when I got it home. I tried to put it in a mental box until a solution occurred to me, yet its presence nagged at my thoughts, along with the worry that I could have been seen taking it.

Other reasons to worry emerged. I learned from a neighbor that Olivia's son, Newt, had bought her house. He was not going to tear it down but renovate it and move in with his new wife. Newt, I feared, had to be familiar with the birdbath. He may have commented to his wife on the birdbath's disappearance and speculated that a workman had taken it, lamenting that he'd been deprived of this memory of his mother and father. My mind ran through the possibilities and various storylines unfurled to me in the middle of the night, beyond my control.

And if I took encountering the wagon as some sort of providence, how should I interpret the circumstance that Newt's daughter, Charlotte, and her family moved into the house directly across the street from ours? She had a husband, who was a lawyer, and two young children, all of whom seemed delightful when I introduced myself at the end of a long walk. They too might recognize the birdbath if they saw it, and I thought it dangerous to fabricate a story that Olivia had given it to me when

Newt could know for a fact that it had stood in her backyard for a long time after her death. Possibly to compensate for my fear of what they might eventually think of me I grew friendly with them, speaking with Charlotte and her son and daughter if they happened to be playing in the yard when I passed by.

I don't know what got into me as I look back on it, but I started to think of Charlotte's kids playing with the wagon. They liked to spend time together outside and seeing them from a window on a cool weekend morning I went out to the garage and uncovered the wagon from under a pile of stuff and pulled it across the street and up their driveway. Charlotte and her kids seemed to love the wagon, and it became part of their play routine. They all waved at me and thanked me when I left, and for a while I felt good seeing them with the wagon, the gift assuaging somewhat my uneasiness about the birdbath.

My feelings changed course as Newt took to showing up regularly at his house to check on its progress. He might know the wagon on sight and ask where they'd gotten it, and I imagined them pointing toward our house and Newt squinting in my direction, the missing birdbath rising from his memory, click, click, click. If Charlotte suspected me of anything, I couldn't tell it. They were friendlier to me than ever, so friendly that I could see it as a natural development that they would come over for a visit and the kids would spill out our back door to play in the yard, their mother joining them and just happening to catch a glimpse of the faux bois birdbath behind the garage. Maybe she'd think nothing of it at the time, but slowly it could come to seem familiar and she could ask Newt to refresh her on what Olivia's birdbath had looked like.

As I continued to picture Charlotte and her kids in my backyard, the thought that I'd given them the wagon unsettled me for many weeks. Had I intended at some level to expose myself? Did I want them to discover the birdbath, which could lead to a confrontation and confession to Newt?

After Newt and his wife moved into their renovated house, I couldn't doubt that they'd all begin to spend extra time together, and a couple of times I saw the kids pulling their wagon down the sidewalk to Newt's. I imagined they'd connected the wagon with the birdbath and were discussing possibilities that inevitably led to me. It became more difficult for me to put my fears aside, and I came to a realization that I could not rest unless I returned the birdbath.

I decided to write Newt a letter telling him how it had all happened, finding the wagon and my mistaken assumptions about the new owners. I asked our yard crew to load the birdbath in their truck and deliver it to Newt's house, place it in the side yard, and put the envelope containing the letter under his front mat. They agreed to make the delivery, and I waited to hear something from Newt.

Within a week, I received a handwritten note in which he assured me that no harm had been done and there was no reason for me to be concerned. We'd all done things we regretted in our lives, he said, and I felt relieved reading his note.

A month later, someone in the neighborhood threw a party that we and many other neighbors were invited to, including Newt and his wife. He had a slight reaction when I introduced myself, his mouth coming open, and I'm sure I blushed as I identified myself as the birdbath lifter. But once he spoke, he couldn't have been more gracious and forgiving, and I said how grateful I was that he hadn't reacted with anger. I didn't tell him how miserable I'd been. I was nervous facing him and kept my talk with him brief.

I went on my way, a fear slowly taking hold that Newt might say something about the birdbath to Vance, who would have been put in the awkward position of asking Newt to explain what I'd done. Another worry was that Newt might not only tell the story to Vance but repeat it in the days ahead to our neighbors. He might come to see it as oddly amusing, especially if he learned that Vance hadn't heard it, and he'd probably include the part about giving Charlotte's kids the wagon.

When we got home, I told Vance. I couldn't stand not to anymore. The story rattled him, and he couldn't sleep.

"You can't do things like that," he said. "You can't know who will hear about it."

I began to take my walks less frequently, but when I did I studied the faces of neighbors I passed to see if I could detect judgment. Vance asked why I'd cut down on my walks and why I sometimes drove to other neighborhoods to take them. I answered that my body was growing old and tired and I wanted to see something different, which opened the door to another subject. Our daughter, Sarah, and her husband had recently moved to a new home in a city four hours south on the interstate. I suggested to Vance that we look for a house there so we could be closer to her. We'd been in our house for decades, I said, and it needed more repairs than we cared to deal with. He liked the idea, so we searched online and in under a month we'd bought a place five minutes from Sarah, the first step in separating from our old neighborhood.

We sold our house quickly, made the move, and haven't been back since. The interstate is too dangerous, loaded with eighteen-wheelers thundering forward at high speeds, swerving as they change lanes, as if threatening retribution to anyone intruding on their territory. We'd rather see new places or stay where we are than return, though my mind does drift back to the birdbath and the question of who's heard the story and who might be telling it.

I've tried to make a clean breast of it in these pages, but I now have misgivings about letting anyone else see them. Yet, concealing my account won't help resolve the episode, which still lingers inside me, like an itch that I can never quite reach.

TUNNEL

I'm in my own house minding my own business when someone knocks on the front door. I hate it when someone knocks because well over half the time it's a nuisance knock, but I make a trip to the peephole to be sure. It's a next-door neighbor we've never met, the man of the family that in the six months since they moved in has caused a nagging sense of encroachment on our peace of mind.

Every weekend this family receives legions of visitors, presumably relatives, who arrive in almost identical SUVs that remain parked in a long line in front of both of our houses for one night, sometimes two. They pour out of the SUVs brandishing smartphones, and a prolonged series of ritual hugging follows, most of the huggers checking their phones over the other person's shoulder. On the way up the walk they seem giddy as they poke their phones and talk at the same time. They gather in the backyard around the pool and play music or sports over their sound system, their noise sucking up all the air around our thoughts whenever we walk out the back door. I haven't taken a look over the eight-foot fence separating our yards, but one recent day I did see my knocking neighbor's pregnant wife and their two four-foot-tall children and the tiny one in the stroller waiting at the school-bus stop, fascinating themselves with their devices. Even the kid in the stroller was vigorously slapping a rectangular screen.

In the interest of fairness and respect, I open the door just as the neighbor raises his fist to knock again. He identifies himself as my neighbor, tells me his name, and apologizes for taking so long to introduce himself. He pauses, so I tell him my name and shake his hand, wondering what he might expect of me. Does he think I should invite him in? I feel no inclination to do so, and I don't call for Denise to come to the door to meet him.

In fact, I dread she'll hear us, walk up from behind and ask him to come in for a chat, so I step out onto the porch and shut the door. I've already forgotten his name, though it's more accurate to say I never remembered it. I don't like the look of him, too self-consciously friendly, a self-serving paternalism that is meant to put me at ease but has the opposite effect, an air of superiority and entitlement he embodies with such purity that I think he must have been born with it. I suspect he may be here to sell me something. He cares nothing about the answers to the questions he asks—where I'm from, how long we've lived in the neighborhood, what I do or used to do for a living, do we have children? For my part I don't care to answer his questions, though I do reply briefly, retired, no kids, and so on. I don't prolong his visit by asking similar questions about him and his family.

"I hope you're not bothered by all the parking we have going on out here on the weekends. We're big believers in family, and we're happy to share our good fortune with them. We feel like we're living the dream and we want our loved ones right here in the dream with us."

He expects these comments to charm me, but the dawning spell is broken when his phone vibrates in his pocket. He excuses himself, lifts the phone out, peeks, pokes something on the phone and puts it away.

"You won't hear that again," he assures me. "I wouldn't want us to be interrupted when I ask you this." He looks me in the eye, hoping I'll smile at him. "This is a little awkward, but believe me, I have generous intentions. Our family loves it here, and both sides, mine and my wife's, parents and brothers and sisters, like to come over so all of us can be together. We cook for one another, and all the kids are there, you must have seen them, generations all under the same roof, all a great pleasure to us, as you can imagine." He pauses again, eyeing me. "The problem is that we're a little crowded, and I'd guess that the number of people we have in our house could at times create some discomfort for you and your wife. I apologize for that, but I've thought of a possible solution. The timing may not be right for you, but I don't know unless I ask, do I? So this is my proposal or question, I'm not sure which word fits best. Have you and your wife ever thought of downsizing? I see the look on your face and I take it that this idea strikes you as out of the blue. I don't mean to be rude, just hear me out for a moment. We'd be willing to make you a more than reasonable offer for your home. We can work together on this, find out what houses are selling for in the area, and we'd add a bonus. That would only be fair since you have a great bargaining advantage here. You own the exact piece of property we want, you don't have a for-sale sign in the yard and you've shown no previous desire to sell. You may be asking yourself why it has to be this property. Because we like it here and we'd prefer not to move again. We don't have the resources to buy some grandiose home, but we need more room to accommodate the family. Unfortunately, the house on our west side has two levels, and we need a one-story house because it's better for our parents. They've got knee and hip replacements to think about, plus the kids running up and down the stairs while checking their phones seems risky to us, they could step off into midair. Our plan is to construct an adjoining hallway between the two houses, one that we could all use to go back and forth in all kinds of weather, and we'd take the fence down between the yards to create sort of a mini-compound for us to roam around in, the pool being complemented by what would be the garden in what is now your backyard. Of course, you can understand how excited we are thinking of the possibilities, but I told Lucille we shouldn't get too far ahead of ourselves, I should go next door and see if any of this has a chance of becoming real. So tell me, are you open to discussing this with your wife? I know it will take time, and we'd have to talk more. You'd need to find another place to live, obviously, and I know excellent people who can help you with that."

Finished, he takes a good look at me, and in his own face I see resentment. It's resentment that I'm not responding to his proposal more openly and graciously, as if putting my desires above his implies a stubborn self-centeredness. The idea that he'll hold a refusal against us makes me imagine throwing him off our little front porch. Instead, I go back in the house and straight to Denise to tell her the story.

"Are you sure that's what he said?" She's on the screened porch reading, music from the other side of the fence intruding into our conversation.

"I know what I heard, and he didn't like it when I didn't reply. Where do they get the presumptuous gall? This must be connected in some way to their proclivity for reproduction."

"You're losing me now."

"He sees us as being past all that and therefore less vital than he is. In his eyes, our standing ranks inherently lower than his. Just think about it."

Denise gazes at me. She occasionally expresses worry that the anesthesia, or some other cause, from my double-hernia surgery has affected my mind. Just then the music coming from next door becomes louder, and our eyes cut toward it.

We haven't heard anything from our neighbor in a week or two, but several fence pickets in the side yard between our houses have been removed and propped up. I show Denise the pickets, which are outside our bedroom, and tell her my suspicions: I think they've had someone over to estimate the cost of an adjoining hallway. She wants me to lower my voice, but I don't care if they overhear me. She waves me back in the house, and I follow her.

"Why would they do that?" she asks when we're inside. "Are you sure he understood you?"

"Why are you asking me again if I'm sure what happened? They simply have no interest in what we want. He may knock on the door again and present us with an offer. Whatever plans they have, we're not included in them, except as ex-neighbors."

This weekend I'm certain that the whole range of generations is over there, likely imagining our place on the inside—what kind of appliances and countertops we have, whether our bathrooms are dated and if the carpet will need to be ripped out.

Denise is telling me the itinerary of a driving trip she's been planning, which will take us through New Mexico, Arizona, Utah, and across Nevada into California. She's made reservations for us in several national parks. As she speaks we hear a distracting noise coming from their house. We go to the fence, and Denise agrees with me that the racket seems to be coming from the part of the house closest to us.

"It sounds like jackhammering," I say.

"They could be looking for a water leak somewhere in

the slab."

"There's no plumber's truck out front."

I go out the back gate and take the short walk down the alley. A white van with no lettering is parked in the driveway and the garage door is up. I see no one and don't want to seem nosy or to get into an angry discussion with anyone. I hurry back and tell Denise about the truck.

"Inconclusive then."

"It's not inconclusive that it's a jackhammer."

"I don't see that it needs to concern us."

I disagree, but I say nothing.

"I'll leave you to it then," she says and goes inside.

I stay near the side fence, my mind working. Eventually I go in and ask Denise if she wants to go to the grocery store with me. As I expect, she says she'll sit in her chair and read.

I stop on my way and buy three baseball bats. I've never owned firearms, though I do keep a bat under our bed. I don't know how I'll explain the bats to Denise, but I want them in different parts of the house, just in case.

Denise is in the kitchen when I get home and she gives me a questioning look when she sees the bats.

"I'll be more comfortable having them around the house."

"Do you imagine we're being invaded?"

"Do you think this is imaginary?"

"I'm sure you're imagining something."

"It doesn't make me wrong."

A few days after the jackhammering I hear knocking. Denise is in the bathroom with the water running and I don't know if she hears it. I tiptoe up to the front door to check the peephole and see our neighbor, straining to keep up his smile. I decide not to speak to him, yet I stay put at the door. He knocks again, looking into the peephole with determination before he walks off.

"Who was that?" Denise asks from behind me.

"It was him. I didn't open up. I've got nothing to say to him."

"Maybe he wanted to make an offer on the house."

"I'm not interested in any offer."

"It wouldn't hurt to listen to what he has to say."

I don't answer her, but I don't like the question left in the silence. Would she consider an offer from him?

Denise returns to the bathroom. I pace around and then

get my utility ladder and carry it out back. I set it up close to the gap in the fence and climb up, steadying myself with a metal post. The ground has been cleared on the other side of the detached part and a chalk outline has been drawn on the brick in the shape of what could become an opening. Our fences connect and run perpendicular to our houses in front, blocking the view of our side yards from the street, but despite that I can't imagine him being reckless enough to begin construction on a hallway. Has he foreseen that I would look over the fence? Is his purpose to make their plan seem more real to me, to harass and intimidate me? Does he want me to envision workmen crashing through the west wall of our bedroom, wearing goggles and hardhats, toting power tools and sledgehammers?

The family gatherings continue, and their noise seems to be getting louder. Denise says it's just my nerves.

I think toward our trip in the weeks ahead. I worry what we'll find when we return if we leave our house unoccupied.

Monday morning I see the family waiting for the school bus, their faces drawn to their phones. As I watch from the front window the wife, Lucille, looks up at me, scowling, her finger suspended in the air.

Late in the afternoon I hear knocking again, and this time I don't go to the door. I'm at my desk, reading a news site on the computer, and soon I hear our door open and Denise's voice. I shut my eyes and tell myself to be patient, to not let anger show in my voice when I speak to her. I imagine his family filing through the under-construction adjoining hallway, rolling luggage in one hand and thumbing messages on smartphones in the other. I see myself waiting with a bat on my shoulder for the first sledgehammer to crash through our bedroom wall.

Denise appears in my doorway holding a slip of paper.

"He's given us the price they'd pay, he and his relatives, and it's more than the house is worth. He says they can give us half the amount in cash."

She comes toward me and tries to show me the number on the paper. I shake my head.

"He made it a point to smile a lot. I didn't like his attitude," she says. "I agree with you, he definitely wants us out."

"What did you tell him?"

"Not a thing, and I didn't look at the number while he was standing there. I don't have any idea of moving anywhere else, especially after listening to him."

"They'll continue to reproduce."

"That will be true wherever they are."

When Denise is in the shower, I take the ladder out and scan their backyard, on the lookout for piles of dirt and rock or elevated levels of dirt in their beds. I see a wheelbarrow and a mound of unearthed dirt and chunks of soiled white rocks by the north side of the fence. I can see no sign of digging anywhere in the yard.

I climb down, take the ladder in and put it away. I pace until the water in the shower goes off. I stop pacing then and go to my study, my thoughts focused on the dirt, the offer, the propped-up pickets, and our vacant house.

Denise's voice startles me. She's standing in the doorway of my study. I'm at my desk, facing the computer, its screen gone black because it's been a while since I touched the keyboard.

"Are you thinking about him?"

"There's a big pile of dirt in their side yard."

"What are you saying?"

"I'd like to know more about the dirt."

"If they had a leak, it may be dirt the plumber dug up."

"Why would the plumber leave it in their yard?"

Denise sighs. Her sigh bothers me, but I can understand

why she'd sigh and can't say anything that would make her want to take it back.

"You think they're digging a tunnel, don't you?"

"I don't know."

"Why would they start the tunnel before making us their offer?"

"He knew I was opposed to selling, but he decided to take his best shot before they dug any farther."

"You're over the top on this, Galen."

"This is our place, not theirs."

I patrol the side yard, listening, sometimes hearing their music and laughter. I can't stay up around the clock, but each night before we turn out the lights I walk the area and drop to my hands and knees, feeling the ground for vibrations. Nothing.

As the trip gets closer, I find it more difficult to sleep. Denise fears we won't be able to enjoy ourselves while we're away. She argues, her agitation showing, that the places we'll visit will remind me of something bigger than the fraught world inside my head. She tells me that if he knocks again, she'll be the one to go to the door. If I go and he says the wrong thing, I might react and our conflict could escalate.

I don't disagree with her.

I wake up in the middle of the night and sit up in bed with such suddenness that I disturb Denise.

"What is it?" she asks.

"I heard a phone ringing. It sounded to me like it was under the house."

"How could it be? There'd be no reception there. Were you asleep when you heard it?"

"I woke up hearing it too. I didn't dream the ring."

I roll out of bed, unsteady on my feet in the dark, and fumble into my pants, shirt, and slippers.

"What are you doing? The tunnel is in your head, Galen. Nothing's there."

I see it as a mistake to underestimate the determination of our neighbor, our enemy. I walk to her side of the bed and drop down. I put my fingertips to the floor and listen.

"I don't feel anything here." I reach under the bed and grab my bat. "I'll check the rest of the house."

"I can't take this anymore, Galen."

As I leave the bedroom, I'm thinking we'll need to cancel

the trip. If we leave the house vulnerable, we could return to find extensive damage or that the rooms have been emptied and our furniture replaced with theirs. Denise will say they wouldn't take it that far, but how can we know for sure what they'd do or try to do? We have rights, sure, but have they shown any respect for them? And how much good can our rights do us when we're not here to defend them?

I decide not to switch on any lights as I prowl. I check the front windows to see how many SUVs are parked along the curb, and I see only one in front of their house. I see no lights on in their house and backyard and hear no activity. The phone that rang has undoubtedly been turned off. I put the bat down and crawl on all fours along the west side of the house. I don't feel vibrations beneath me or hear hacking, but I picture them underground, digging their way toward us and finally up. If someone's head pops through our floor, I hope he'll be the one leading the break-in. I'll pick up my bat and turn on a light. I'll let him get a look at what hit him.

CONTACT

I don't know why, but until I went to her door our neighbor Marie hadn't spoken to me in more than a year. I usually only see her in passing, and when I do she keeps her head low and doesn't look at me. If I say hello she ignores me. My wife, Rose, claims Marie sometimes speaks to her but doesn't say much, small talk, nothing more. Marie's husband, Harris, has remained as friendly as ever.

A couple of Sunday mornings ago I went out for my run and noticed two newspapers in their front yard. I thought they must be out of town and either forgot or didn't take the time to stop the paper. I jogged to the papers, picked them up and carried them to the porch. I put the papers behind the flowerpot in the corner, neighborly thing to do. Their house has two narrow vertical windows on each side of the front door, just like ours, and as I looked up I saw Marie about twenty feet ahead, apparently walking from the kitchen to the den or the bedroom. She saw me looking in and stopped. There I was, staring at her in my singlet and running shorts. I resisted an impulse to turn away and instead knocked on the door with the idea of giving her an explanation. She didn't react but continued watching me. Did she fear what I'd do or say, did it annoy her that a person she didn't want to speak to in the first place was knocking on her door? Were my legs, shoulders, and armpits more than she cared to be faced with? I knocked again and saw her start toward me, muttering to herself. She turned three bolt locks, high, low, and middle, swung the door open. May I help you? she said, though I could tell she had no desire to help me at all. I told her about the papers and pointed at them. Both of those papers were delivered this morning, she said, and it's only half past nine. One we only get on Sunday. Are we obligated to bring them in before a certain time? I saw no need to answer her question. I wondered if Harris might appear behind her and ask what we were talking about. But I didn't see or hear him, and I guessed he wasn't there. Is that all? she asked. She looked me up and down with suspicion, but something more was in her look. I thought she wanted to hit me or grab my balls and give them a yank. I almost groaned out loud imagining she wouldn't let go.

I ran away from her. I headed up the street, afraid she might still be watching me, and after less than a block, head and stomach grinding, I reversed course and went home. Rose asked why I'd come back so soon, and I filled her in about the newspapers and talking to Marie at her door.

You told her the reason, Rose said. That's all you could do.

I don't know if she believed me.

Why wouldn't she?

I have a feeling this is not over, I said.

Nothing happened until the next Sunday. I'd just gotten up, on my way to the kitchen, teeth freshly brushed, free day ahead, time with the paper, maybe a movie, Rose out of town on business, freedom to talk out loud to the traffic in my head, freedom to sit in my chair and cry, no explanations or answers due to anyone, little or no direct human contact—but wait. There she was, Marie dressed in running clothes, red shorts, hair in an arching ponytail, peering through the vertical window next to the front door, holding my newspaper up for me to see, not smiling, daring me to come for it, light rain falling behind her. It took me a minute to kick into gear, to process her appearance. I knew she'd think I was a coward if I didn't open the door. What in the world would she say, what ideas were jerking her around?

I opened it. She thumped one end of the newspaper in a wet plastic wrapper against my chest. I took the paper from her hand.

Not running today? she asked.

It's raining.

Pussy, she said. She leaned toward me, confiding, angry. Harris is out of town, as you may know, but if you show up over there you won't leave in one piece.

She ran across our yards, back to her house. I went inside and looked out the window, fearing she might get it into her head to return. Why did she tell me Harris was out of town? Did she know that Rose was also away? Things were normal between Rose and me, but did Marie think I knew or suspected something? Was I off on the wrong track? What basis did I have to answer any of these questions?

I wanted to talk with her, ask her questions, though she'd made it clear I shouldn't go over there. Did something in her want to talk? Did she have mixed feelings? Did she think I had another reason for showing up at her door? Human contact was the source of most suffering, so where did this sentiment come from about needing contact with people to be happy?

I called her number but hung up after one ring, unable to gather my thoughts. Less than a minute later the phone rang, and I let it ring three times before I picked it up.

Was that you? Marie said.

Several words tried to come out at the same time, all of

them colliding and creating an inarticulate sound.

Why did you call? she asked.

I didn't know where to begin or what I should ask. I feared bringing up something that could be off base.

What were you doing on my porch? she asked.

That was exactly the question I wanted to ask her.

I already told you why, I said.

Do you want to tell me something?

I wanted to know if she wanted to tell me something. I didn't answer, too many disordered thoughts racing in my head.

Are you having suspicions?

Again, exactly what I wanted her to tell me. I didn't know what to say.

Your brain is a wilderness, she said. You're wasting my time.

She hung up on me, leaving me frustrated, my mouth open, nothing that could be called a word coming out of it.

I sat at the kitchen table and tried to think. What did I know about whatever was upsetting me? I couldn't answer the question. Marie had done this to me, getting even for some reason that made sense to her though not to me. I picked up the phone and called her back.

You again, she said.

Please tell me what you know.

I'm not telling you anything.

CONNECT

We were in a Mexican restaurant at the mall, and my husband, as is his habit, had his eyes on everything except me. I still had half an enchilada left, but Boyd's empty plate had already been removed and he'd ground through all the tortilla chips and salsa on the table, leaving his eyes and mind free to survey the room. His attention was drawn to the occupants of a booth across and at a slight angle from ours. He could see them better than I could. I peeked back and saw a man and woman, presumably married, and an intellectually disabled boy, the boy seated on the man's side, which may have appealed to Boyd. The three of them were a picture of happiness, talking and smiling and enjoying one another. If the boy was their son, they'd likely been married at least ten years, and I admit I couldn't help comparing how they seemed to how we were after fifteen years.

I'm telling the waiter I'm paying for their meals, Boyd said.

I put my fork down in my plate and before I could say a word Boyd cut me off.

Don't start with it, he said. There's no reason to think it

should make them uncomfortable. I'm going to go tell them I'm proud of them and it's a pleasure to see them here together.

He rose and walked the few steps to their booth. I didn't want the family to sense my opposition, so I waited a minute and then turned to show them my face, trying not to appear disagreeable. The man seemed to be resisting Boyd, yet Boyd kept talking, persuading, saying something about *dinner*, something about *glad to have you*, his hands moving in front of him. The man, his smile fading, glanced over at me, and I looked away so he wouldn't see my discomfort. When the waiter came by for my plate, I pulled a credit card from my purse and gave it to him. I could hear Boyd telling them he was proud of them, a sentiment he loved repeating to strangers, and I cringed and quit listening to him.

The waiter brought the credit-card bill, and I signed and handed it back at about the same time Boyd returned. I got up and told him we were ready to go and both of us smiled at the family. The woman met my eyes, possibly wondering how I felt about what Boyd had proposed or estimating the level of suffering that might be revealed in the face of the woman married to him. I didn't like the invasiveness of her stare. Whatever was in my eyes was none of her business. I could have been wrong about her, but I wasn't going to her booth to find out.

I could tell the conversation hadn't gone as well as Boyd had hoped. We exited the restaurant in a hurry and walked out into the bustle of the mall, Boyd not making eye contact with anyone. His face had closed, and I knew from experience that it had closed specifically to me.

I changed my mind about picking up their check and asked them to our house for dinner, he said, and the second I mentioned it he looked at you and his face changed. He didn't feel welcome.

I don't want strangers coming over for dinner, I said, and I don't assume strangers have any desire to connect with me.

People are going to stay strangers to you if you refuse to trust them.

Why is it my fault they turned you down? Maybe they felt hesitant because they don't have the slightest idea who we are. They may have felt vulnerable having you at their table, trespassing on their time together. What did they say when you told them you were proud of them? Did they ask you why?

You object to me showing goodwill toward people we don't know. Don't you see what a limited philosophy that is?

It comes out every time I attempt a connection or show some generosity. Your voice is always arguing inside my head and I can't get it out.

Boyd hadn't once laid eyes on me since we'd left the restaurant and now he picked up his pace and walked ahead of me. He began noticing his surroundings again, some of it for my benefit, I suspected, setting an example of openness for me. He stepped onto an escalator and I watched him go all the way up without showing any interest in whether I was following. So I didn't. I couldn't stomach thinking he took pleasure in punishing me, dragging me around behind him, treating me worse than he treated strangers. He'd driven us to the mall, but I had a key in my purse and I could go to the car and drive home alone.

For the time being I decided to watch him from a distance and see how long it would take for him to miss me. I had an idea he was headed to a department store at the other end of the mall. He'd planned to go there to check out a sale. I took a stairway up to the next level and saw him far ahead on the walkway to the left side, his head turning in every direction except behind him.

As he neared the department store I saw him stop at the window of a men's clothing store. He apparently expected me to walk up and stand beside him because after a moment he turned to look for me, seeming disturbed I wasn't there. I hid in a doorway, watching him squint, his eyes scanning the people coming toward him. He started back to me, on the alert for my image while still smiling at passersby, greeting a family with a wave, asking those who smiled back at him how they were doing. I'd seen it all many times, some people giving him a blank look when he smiled or waved and others ignoring him. I saw a woman with broad shoulders and long blond hair abruptly step toward him and point. She was several inches taller than Boyd and I gathered she didn't like the way he'd looked at her or the way he'd smiled. Boyd tried to reason with her, keeping his smile up, but she wasn't interested and was making her view clear to him. When she moved away from Boyd, he said something that appeared to be conciliatory; she pivoted and made an angry comment. Boyd didn't accept her anger. He took a step, and she stiffened and stood face to face with him as he debated with her, I presumed, about being more open to others.

Then a man came out of a store and saw the argument, and he came toward them and joined forces with the woman. He was bigger than she was and Boyd backed up, though he refused to stop talking.

I felt no urge to go to his aid and imagined the man

picking him up and throwing him over the railing to the lower level. I could peek down and see Boyd's cracked head bleeding on the shiny floor tiles below. The couple didn't murder him, but they made some hostile or perhaps threatening comment and left Boyd standing with his open hands in front of him, unable to comprehend their attitude.

He resumed his search for me, and I decided to go to the car and drive home. It made me furious to think he'd imagined me trailing behind him, and after what I'd witnessed I couldn't walk next to him without fearing another altercation with someone who didn't care to be browbeaten with his openness and generosity.

I walked faster than usual, putting Boyd out of my mind. I pushed through the exit door and walked down the wrong row in the parking lot, then saw our car on the row to my left. I walked between some cars, and as I dug the keys out of my purse I heard Boyd's voice calling my name. I saw him wave and smile.

I guess we got separated and you couldn't find me, he said as he approached. I thought you might be at the car.

I separated us, I told him. I let you go.

You were going to leave me here?

You walked away from me. Why shouldn't I?

I've been looking for you, he said, his smile gurgling down the drain.

I saw you. You didn't look that long.

You were watching? Why didn't you come to me?

I thought I might interfere with your openness.

Did you see that couple nearly attack me?

Maybe they thought you were too aggressive and argumentative.

I thought they were aggressive and argumentative, he said. But let's not have this out in the parking lot.

Why not? Why be closed to others? Or we could go back in the mall and find the couple and ask them over for dinner. I'd like to hear what they have to say, get to know them. I think we could forge a lasting friendship.

Should we get in the car?

Do you promise not to talk?

Hey, is that guy bothering you? I heard someone shout.

I saw the aggrieved couple about to get in their car. Instead, they slammed their doors and came at us with an air of menace, their anger converging on Boyd. The man had obviously spent a lot of time pumping weights, thick neck and shoulders, bulging veins. A large tattoo surrounded the bottom of his neck, continuing underneath his shirt, and tattoos of barbed wire wound around his hands and forearms. The woman also carried the aura of a physical type and looked strong enough to inflict damage if she chose to.

You get around, don't you? the man said to Boyd.

This is a misunderstanding. She's my wife.

Is that true? he asked me.

More or less, I said.

Which is it? the woman asked. More? Or less?

Less, I answered.

Let's not butt in here, the man said in a lower voice. Let's back off. He's not accosting a stranger.

The woman's mood remained the same.

I'm watching you, she yelled at Boyd as they walked back to their car.

Did you enjoy that? Boyd asked.

I don't like you bringing angry strangers into my life. It makes me sick.

Then why say that to them?

I wanted to.

I don't get it.

Right.

He couldn't think of anything to say, and I enjoyed his silence. I pressed the button on my key to unlock the car. Boyd drifted to the passenger side, and I took the wheel.

HOST

Don't get mad, I'm trying to explain something to you. I know you think I should leave the subject alone, respect his silence, but how do you interpret his behavior? I've gone over every second we've spent with this guy, the mystery neighbor who won't open his mouth, looking for some perspective. You dropped a dinner invitation in his mailbox asking him to reply to us by phone or email, and he waited more than a week, only two days till the date, before sending an email that said Y. You took this to mean Yes, though I thought it could be short for Why. Now I think he may have meant to suggest both. He didn't add a question mark, true, and it turned out he did show up at our door on time with a bottle of wine in hand, which doesn't seem to fit with the bigger picture. Maybe he saw the wine as a substitute for a facial expression because he did not bring one of those. I went to the door, greeted him warmly, he extended the wine to me, I thanked him and asked him in. The chihuahuas were behind me barking, his eyes resting on them, and it was clear he wouldn't take a step into our house until the chihuahuas had been removed. So I set the wine down and picked up a dog in each arm and carried them to our bedroom and shut the door. He hadn't moved from the doorway when I returned. I again asked him to enter and he took a long step, as if over a chasm stretching between the outside and inside. I urged him to keep going, but he waited until I'd closed the front door and walked past him.

In the den, he didn't speak to the Halls, didn't seem to know they were there, though I think I remember that you rated a glimpse. He sat like a statue all through drinks, not touching his water or the appetizers, and at dinner his mouth never moved except to eat his vegetables. Unfortunately, he didn't tell us beforehand that he doesn't eat meat. And soon after dinner he stood, gave me a nod and then vanished into the night. That may sound dramatic for a man who embodies the absence of drama, but those are the words that came to mind when I opened the door and released him. The Halls didn't say anything about him after he left, but I'd bet that on their way home they commented on his apparent lack of interest in other people.

Against my wishes, you invited him to a second dinner party, only two months after the first one, though we received no thank you for the first dinner. You said he smiled at you, barely, one day when you saw him in his driveway, and you chose to see this smile as a form of gratitude. You emailed him and, as you know, close to a week later you got another Y from him. It annoyed me to see how happy you were that he'd exerted himself enough to send us one letter. Again I wondered if the letter implied a question, but as you predicted he made another appearance with another bottle of wine, the chihuahuas barking at him from behind our bedroom door.

He repeated himself almost perfectly that second night, all the way down to wearing the same clothes, though I'm not sure if he wore the same socks. Not a word came out of his mouth, not a smile, nothing showing in his face, until at dinner I asked him about his painting.

What can you tell us about your work? I asked, and right away I could tell he wasn't inclined to respond. I brought you up on a search engine, and I was puzzled by the level of abstraction in what I read and in the images I looked at.

I admit that I wanted to disrupt the purity of his silence and to force my way into him. I was sick of him sitting there eating our food and refusing to even look at us. I know you don't want to see it that way, and, yes, I am making an effort to see it from his side. You think he could be a nice guy and doesn't know how to show it, but where's the evidence? I think you're dreaming up an inner person for him because you think he's interesting, an artist and all that, and you think he's good looking and he probably thinks you're good looking. What does that have to do with what kind of person he is and whether he thinks we're beneath him, small people living in a tiny, unexceptional world that can't compare with the layered world of abstraction and significance he thinks he lives in?

Anyway, what was his answer to my question? He came out with one word, you'll remember. Complex, he said in a quiet voice and then he was done, implying in my opinion that if he were to discuss his work further, we'd be incapable of understanding him. He let me go on staring at him, over-chewing his next bite, making it impossible for him to speak until he'd swallowed without breaking decorum, as if he gave a flick about decorum. Wouldn't you think he'd speak at a dinner party if he cared about decorum? I can't imagine, and neither can you, going to two dinner parties in a row without addressing the hosts or anyone else who happened to be there. You can't deny that, can you?

I'm not through, just hold on, I'm going to say what I want. After cleaning up we went to bed tired and without a thank you from the painter. I started to talk about him, but you cut me off and said you were tired of hearing it. You insisted I couldn't know why he refused to speak and you wanted me to shut up about him. Outwardly I respected your wishes; inside I went on talking and thrashing, burrowing into his silence, asking what was inside it. The more I thought about his radical nothingness, which seemed to be directed at us, the more upset I got, and as I lay awake I hit upon the idea of confronting him. I'd go to his house and knock on his door and stand there looking at him, wondering if he'd ask me in. What if he didn't? He might slam the door in my face or simply look back at me. I got so wound up in my thoughts that I couldn't get to sleep. I felt judged, and of course this was all in my mind, but isn't some judgment of us implicit in his attitude? The longer I saw myself languishing in front of him at his door the more foolish I felt. There could be no pretense of a connection between us, and my silence seemed pathetic while his seemed somehow majestic, almost God-like. You'll say I made myself feel this way and you'd be right. But you have thoughts about people that make you feel good or bad about yourself, don't you? Is that all your own doing? Aren't we entitled to a semblance of respect from him?

I got out of bed feeling like an idiot, still clinging to the idea of going to his door, humiliating myself in all versions I could imagine but determined to evoke a response from him. It was a Sunday morning, huge newspaper, and I read in the arts section about a gallery show, abstract painter, decent review, perfect, something our wonderful friend might be interested in. As I chewed my cereal, I imagined walking between our houses with my section of newspaper and asking him if he'd seen the article, just a pretext, but I needed more than a stupid look on my face and nowhere to go from there. At around ten I grabbed the arts section and didn't say anything to you about what I planned to do. I knew you'd be against it, and you would have been right to discourage me, I'm not blind to that point, yet I felt driven to do this thing that in some way I knew was a bad idea.

I knocked on his door, no answer, and then I rang the bell. After a minute or so I heard his footsteps, and he opened the door and looked at me with what could have been a hint of surprise. He didn't have much of a reaction, but he did seem to expect me to explain myself. I said hello and he did not reply. I let the pause hang for a moment, hoping he'd weaken and mutter a greeting. He didn't. I held up the arts section and pointed to the review of the art show. Had he seen the article? His head moved, less than half a nod, end of pretext, and he moved the door slightly toward me, already trying to cover me up, suggesting we were finished unless I had more to add. I stared into his eyes, and though I resented his blank face I was strangely conscious of my hypocrisy, trying to know what was inside him and what he saw when he looked at me yet not wanting him to imply anything with the indifference of his stare. I imagined lunging at him, grabbing him by the head, taking him down. I know you don't like hearing this, but listen. Did he think I was nothing? Is that what he saw in me? That's the way he acted and always has. Not that it makes what I did or wanted to do right, but it seemed he'd put these self-demeaning thoughts in my head. I felt demoralized by his presence and unworthy of the response I craved. I asked myself why he would care to invite me in. What would we have said to each other? It was painfully true that neither of us would have spoken a meaningful word. Would that have been because of me? I turned away from him, and his door was closed and locked before I could take a step off his porch.

I can still see his face, its failure to acknowledge me except as a rudimentary object cluttering an otherwise empty space. I've thought about this, trying to understand, and here's what I've come up with. What I see when he looks at me is my own thoughts. It's me looking down from his face. I put my thoughts there or, more precisely, created the illusion they were there, but only because he wanted me to. He wouldn't take the time to actively disrespect or judge me. He wouldn't bother to indulge in that level of destructive intimacy. What he's done is much less than that and therefore more deviously and complexly insulting. He's led me to see myself in the reduced and pathetic form that I imagined he saw me, and he must have done it with obliterating intent. Why else would he come to our house for dinner and not speak? And his end of the unspoken conversation, through the walls of its silence, tells us more. Do you understand what I'm saying? Am I getting through to you? This is the way he wants it, or as he would think of it, doesn't want it. If he spoke, this would be his final word. He doesn't want to know us and doesn't want us to know the first thing about his existence and he'd probably prefer that we didn't know he exists at all. It's so obvious, I can't see it any other way.

DUE

I had a question I couldn't answer. What in the hell was Davenport feeding the bug up his ass? Ever since I'd loaned him money, he hadn't been the same with me, though admittedly we had an issue unconnected with the debt he could not repay. For years Davenport suffered with longing for my wife, Em, and after she left me, he couldn't find it in his heart to forgive me for losing her.

After being let go from a string of jobs, Davenport was often unshaven and unwashed and tended to wear the same shirt for up to a week. On occasion I thought I'd caught a whiff of him in the air, but when I turned and looked I did not see him. As long as I'd known him, he'd expressed grievances against any person or group with power over him, including his bosses and "the government," and I'd become a favorite target of his umbrage, a close-at-hand example of the forces tormenting him. Yet I'd done nothing to torment Davenport, and I was at the end of my wits with his harassment.

I relaxed in the evenings by enjoying a drink, and one place I sometimes frequented was a hotel bar a block or so from my building. The trouble was that Davenport knew I went there, and one evening he brushed against me before I was served and took a stool beside me. The bartender soon set my drink down and asked Davenport if he wanted anything. "Not yet," he said, though he and I knew he had no money to spare for a drink. He eyed mine, his tongue moving inside his mouth, and sat quietly for a moment, letting his presence sink in.

"I have a confession to make, Richard," he began. "I think I may have damaged your marriage. Em must have known I loved her far more than you did. I saw her and listened to her in ways you never could and that must have weighed on her and caused her to see you as deficient in many ways. She didn't love me, much to my regret, but she must have felt she deserved to be loved by someone who valued her more than you did. She found someone more worthy of her, not surprisingly, and decided she'd be devaluing herself if she failed to repudiate your neglect and dump you. Like a fool, you let her get away, and you probably saw nothing lacking in you to explain what you'd lost. To be able to touch that skin and not have it mean everything to you. It's beyond me how you could let her go. I can imagine what you must have put her through, because my feelings for her allow me to feel her pain, just as much as if you'd done something to me.

You make me angry, and I resent the pain you've brought to my life and Em's. The least you can do is buy me a drink. If you think it's right, you can add the cost to my tab."

"Please stop talking," I replied. "If I buy you a drink you'll only sit here and make me listen to more. Why would I want that? Don't talk to me about touching Em's skin. I don't need you to help me suffer with this. Can't you just leave me alone?"

"That question summarizes the goal of your life. All you really want is to be left alone, in this case to sit here by yourself with your self-centered thoughts. You'd like to move on and forget her, but I don't delude myself I can let her go so easily. I wish for her happiness more than you do."

"You can't know that. One thing I know is that either you're leaving or I'm leaving."

"I'm not going anywhere. I'm ordering a drink. We both need one, Richard, can't you see that?"

He waved at the bartender and ordered a vodka and tonic.

"I'm not paying for it," I said to the bartender, "and this man has no money."

I downed what was left of my drink, flipped some money on the bar, and hopped off my stool. Davenport canceled his drink order and followed me out. Rather than try to elude him, I stopped and stared into his face. He wasn't fazed and would have stood there for as long as I chose. What else did he have to do? I went on my way, Davenport on my heels or pulling even with me to make comments in my ear.

"Do you think running away changes anything?"

And: "Do you think you can ever be really alone?"

And: "Do you think you can erase a woman like Em from your memory or ever get over her?"

"What does it have to do with you?" I asked him. "What do you think *I* have to do with you? Is it because I gave you a loan? If you can't stand owing me money, why be angry at me about it?"

At that question he dropped back, his footsteps no longer dogging me. I entered my building, relieved to be safe from him yet cursing him on my way up in the elevator, talking over images of decking him or pushing him into oncoming traffic. I tried to shut myself up and clear my mind, but Davenport went on yakking in my head.

I abandoned the hotel bar as a destination and considered other places where I could enjoy a drink. I chose the bar at a Thai restaurant blocks away. Whenever I'd been to the restaurant it had been almost empty and I'd never seen a soul sitting in the bar, which was around a corner and not visible from the street. Before leaving my building I peered out the window to see if I could spot Davenport. I emerged, looking both ways, and walked to the Thai place, several times glancing behind me.

The bar was unoccupied, four empty stools, two small booths along a short wall, poor lighting, a muted TV showing a football game. I went to the bar, ordered, and then carried my drink to a booth, facing so that I could see anyone who entered. I enjoyed the stillness, the soothing drink and the ice tinkling in the glass.

A few minutes later I heard Davenport speaking to the host about meeting a friend. Did he have a way of tracking me through my phone? He rounded the corner and plopped down opposite me, his head lowered, suggesting he'd rather not lay eyes on me. If so, why had he come? Whether I got up and walked out or sat and listened, I'd feel at his mercy either way.

"You make me sick," he began, looking up.

"Please tell me more."

"Last time, you asked what you and Em have to do with me. Do you realize how small-minded that question is? Should I limit my concerns to things that only have to do with me? Can't I be angry on behalf of Em? I love her, and whatever affects her also affects me. I wish you could share in my compassion for her."

"I have a proposal. If you agree never to speak to me again, I will erase your debt. The agreement would include any form of communication. Leave me alone, and you don't owe me a penny."

"I can't be bought off, Richard. I won't take the bait. I know you hate me and imagine doing things to me to make me be quiet. Did you think I didn't know? You can't use my debt to buy some phony peace of mind you believe is due to you. You wouldn't be giving up a thing by erasing it, anyway, because you know I'm never paying you. Do you think I'm stupid enough to take a deal like that? I'm insulted in more ways than one. You would never have loaned me the money if Em hadn't urged you to. That debt serves as a memory of her kindness. You can't just snap your fingers and make that disappear."

"Forgive me, I thought the debt was hanging over you. You do seem to be implicitly asking me for something. You seem to want to be on the receiving end from me, as if you're reversing the charges. What do you want? Is all your talk supposed to take me somewhere? Or do you see it as ongoing punishment?"

"Your manipulations won't change what I think. Every word out of your mouth connives to silence and obliterate me.

I'm not surprised. My love for Em overshadowed yours, and you can't live with that."

"What would it take for you to get even with me?"

"It's impossible," he said. "This has to do with who you are."

"So why do you bother? Do you think Em wants this?"

"Em is through with you. This is what you deserve. Does anyone else care enough to deliver that message? I don't think so."

"How much do you owe to other people? I'm not offering to pay it off. Just asking."

"You know that's none of your business."

"Does it increase your sense of desperation? I'm trying to understand you."

"You never will."

He stood then, huffing some disdainful air toward me. After I heard the door close I ordered another drink.

I did not see Davenport for a while, but memories of him unsettled me and he spoke to me in my sleep, asking me to pay him back as he touched Em's skin. How could I know if he knew what he wanted from me or understand the hellish world he'd made for himself?

One morning I was eating breakfast at a Waffle House when I saw Davenport looming at the window alongside my booth. I could see he'd taken a beating. His shoulders drooped, one more than the other, his face bruised and scabbed, his eyes swollen almost shut, a bandage stuck to his neck. He gazed at me through the glass, as if making an assessment. Who could guess what he read or thought he read in my face? I expected him to come in and let loose a torrent of abuse. Instead, he turned and limped away.

He dropped out of sight after that, and for some time I imagined he'd appear suddenly at my side. I contacted Em to see if she'd seen him, but she said she hadn't and I believed her. Where was he? The image of his beaten face still came to me, but it left me angry and unsatisfied. His voice remained, humiliating me, echoing through me.

I can never pay him back.

SHEPHERD

Apart from what I'd said to our acquaintance and apart from what I said about it to Shepherd, it bothered me that Shepherd assumed I was lying when I denied what I'd said, and it bothered me that he was in effect lying to me by pretending to believe me. Where did he get off presuming to hold the moral high ground while lying to me for lying to him? Should I feel ashamed for lying as he luxuriated in his low opinion of me? I could see that he wanted me to know he knew I was lying, despite his silent pretense of believing me, and was looking to me for tacit acknowledgment that I knew he knew. He sneered, just enough to make me notice. I asked Shepherd why he'd asked what I'd said if he had no intention of believing me, but he refused to reply. He didn't want to come out and say he'd taken pleasure in listening to me lie, in verifying I lacked the courage to admit what I'd said to our acquaintance about him. Shepherd wanted to tell himself he should feel no obligation to tell the truth to a liar. I believe he preferred silence to saying something that would escalate tension. It would never have occurred to Shepherd, his imperial highness, that I had similar reasons for lying to him. Shepherd didn't want any part of an angry conflict, all he wanted to do was sneer. He liked sitting in the observation chair in his head, gazing down from his lofty perch on the world sprawling and scrambling beneath him. At that point I decided I wouldn't sit still for Shepherd's attitude or his bullshit. I told him I wasn't the one who'd made the statements he thought I'd lied about. Our acquaintance had made them, though I'd sort-of agreed with what he'd said, and now he wouldn't own up to it and had deflected the words from his mouth by claiming I'd said them. Shepherd immediately discounted my story, asking me why our acquaintance would deflect words Shepherd would never have heard. I answered that he might have feared I'd go to Shepherd and repeat them, and he wanted to tell his version before I told mine. Or it could have been because I'd slept with his girlfriend, though this was the first time I'd had any reason to think he might have been aware of it. Perhaps he wanted to take revenge by turning people against me, I suggested to Shepherd. All this was a lie, and I wasn't actually sure if our acquaintance still had a girlfriend. Shepherd kept sneering to himself, and I wondered if he was thinking of sharing the story with our acquaintance for a laugh. I told Shepherd he could check it out if he wanted to, but I didn't see why our acquaintance would choose to embarrass himself with a confession, especially since he could imagine what his girlfriend might have said to me about him, which I in turn could have recounted to Shepherd. Easier for him to attribute the whole story to me, I went on, and implicitly deny that his girlfriend and I had ever spoken. Shepherd told me not to worry, that he saw no reason to ask anyone about it, implying I should be the one to worry and not our acquaintance. I imagined him going home and pouring himself drink after drink and laughing his ass off at me. But would he show me his true face? No, not Shepherd. He didn't play it that way. He wanted to shame me into silence by simply letting on that he knew every word I said was a lie, to revel in his superiority until I lowered my head and skulked off to my hidey-hole. I couldn't accept letting Shepherd maneuver me into some cowardly retreat. I offered to drive him over to our acquaintance's house so we could find out together what he'd fess up to, and if Shepherd agreed to my dare I didn't mind standing right up and calling our acquaintance a liar. Why should I care about this acquaintance when he'd repeated what I'd said about Shepherd? I had no friendship with him and only spoke to him in an offhand way, though we'd known each other for years. Shepherd said he didn't think we needed to drive to our acquaintance's house, and

I asked him what he meant, thinking his comment suggested he could tell I'd been lying without having to prove it. I replied that it surprised me he'd back down when he was so sure he was right about everything. What was he afraid of? I asked him. Shepherd said it wouldn't be right to involve our acquaintance's girlfriend in the discussion. She could be at home or she could find out we'd dropped by and mentioned her name in an unflattering way. He avoided directly accusing me of lying to him, though his meaning was clear enough. I told him that his real reason for refusing to drive to our acquaintance's was that he didn't want to lower himself to participate in what he presumed to know was a narrative I'd fabricated. He thought his way of seeing things was superior to mine, I accused him, and since we began talking his whole surreptitious purpose had been to lower my standing and raise his. Did he ever consider the cynicism of such an approach? Why ask people questions when you don't intend to believe them? I asked Shepherd again, my tone more demanding this time. He did not answer my question, and if he had I probably wouldn't have believed him, but he tilted his head up and said: Okay, let's go over there. You can follow me. I suspected Shepherd suspected I'd chicken out, but I didn't. I had only a vague sense of where our acquaintance lived so I raised no objection to following him as we walked to our cars. Shepherd must have relished the thought of exposing me as a liar, and he must have calculated that no harm would be done to anyone except me. He knew the acquaintance better than I did and may even have considered him to be a friend, and he may therefore have known his girlfriend well enough to guess she'd have nothing to do with me. I fumed at Shepherd as I drove, and I imagined him imagining that he might finally crack on our acquaintance's front porch and laugh himself into a frenzy. I was relieved to see no cars parked in front of the house when we arrived, and I hoped no one would be at home. Shepherd hopped out of his car and bounded up to the front door. I walked at a normal pace, and the moment I set foot on the small porch he rang the bell. I sensed he was judging me, waiting for me to flee the scene, too chastened to ever show my face again. The girlfriend answered and greeted Shepherd, who stood only a couple of feet from the door. He asked if our acquaintance was at home, and she said he wasn't. She then looked at me more closely and flinched, the sight of me coming as a shock, her eyes returning to Shepherd, her mouth opening but not finding any words. Do you know this man? Shepherd asked. Not for a while, but I do know him, she admitted. She asked Shepherd why he'd come. Did he want to make trouble? She didn't appreciate being confronted and she didn't see what anyone could gain by dragging me in front of her face. Shepherd appeared at a loss without his condescension to protect him. He apologized to her and said he'd made a mistake. He didn't know she knew me, though I'd told him she did. He'd thought I'd lied and he wanted to settle the matter, clear her name. So now my name is not cleared, is that what you're saying? she asked Shepherd. I liked her and wondered why I'd ever let her go. We'd only been together one time for a few hours, but I thought I could be excused for letting myself get carried away with Shepherd's defeat. I could stand on the porch and claim my hands were clean, while Shepherd couldn't possibly dig himself out of his hole. She berated him for using her as a test subject in his improvised lie-detector test. Why didn't you call first, she asked, because it would be more dramatic this way? Shepherd took a jittery step away from her, stumbling on the welcome mat, and swore never to mention our visit to anyone. He knows, she replied, and they both looked at me as if I were no one to be trusted. Did they have to make me squirm just because they were? I held up my hands and then put my forefinger straight up against my lips, a signal known by everyone. I wouldn't talk. Yet, they didn't seem satisfied. Both of them were on the defensive, and I could see it and smell it on them. Shepherd must have feared I'd take pleasure in getting back at him by spreading the story around. I couldn't think at the moment who I'd tell it to, but if provoked I could consider the possibilities, including online options. On the other hand, I had nothing against her particularly, except that she kept glaring at me with contempt. As she saw it, I'd blabbed about her without any reason to, and I couldn't explain that I'd done so without knowing she was the one I was blabbing about. Determined to stay silent and thereby maintain some distance from a situation embarrassing to both of them, I vigorously shook my head and bowed to her. She thanked me, at least seeming to accept my unstated promise. I walked away then, hoping Shepherd would chase after me and do some groveling, and even though he didn't, he was stuck with the girlfriend, repeating an abject apology that would be unlikely to reduce her disdain for him. I left Shepherd to wonder how much of what I'd said could be true and whether he should question our acquaintance about who'd said what and whether the girlfriend would reveal to our acquaintance that Shepherd had appeared with a man from a one-night misstep she'd like to forget. And the idea angrily crept up on me that I needn't keep my promise not to speak, not after all Shepherd had put me through, and neither of them should expect me to withhold my version of the story when they'd probably be telling their own versions to justify themselves. I couldn't remember what had happened between the girlfriend and me, but whatever it was she'd tell it in a way that would put her in the most favorable light. It made no sense for me to trust two people who saw themselves as above me, to put myself at a disadvantage by remaining silent. I couldn't ignore or forget the way Shepherd had looked down at me. Consequences had roots, and it wasn't my problem if they failed to understand that.

SELF-SERVICE

Out of the hotel room, early evening, headed to a movie, wife too tired to come, didn't want to thrash around a strange city looking for a movie theater, all day in the rental car, trouble getting the windshield wipers and the fan to work, wrong turn here, wrong turn there, she'd rather have a nap. Street long and narrow and windy, high walls of concrete and brick on both sides, wind blowing grit in my face and teeth. Walls seem to lean in, my chest tight, breath short, lower my head and keep walking into the wind, peeking up to see if the corner's nearing, right turn not yet visible. Press ahead, socks sweaty, toes bumping the ends of my shoes, leaning forward, coughing, licking my teeth to unseal the grit, turning my head and spitting it out. No one else on the street, few doors or windows, the block goes on and on, but it does come to an end, it cannot stretch to infinity, corner up ahead, breath coming easier at the turn, see the theater, enter, man inside wearing a navy blazer and a tie, tells me the tickets are self-service, keep going around the corner, machine on the wall of the building. Self-sufficiency, he says and gives me a wink, hallmark of maturity and adulthood. Back outside, find my way, another right turn, machine on the wall, short line, check my wallet, all of us shrinking into ourselves, trying to hide from the wind. Front of the line, instructions on the machine, press the button labeled with the name of your movie. It wants eight dollars, but no five or ones in my wallet, not even a ten, the machine doesn't like my crisp twenty, line building up behind me, bill goes part way in, then back out. Guy behind me pushes a button on the machine, says try again. The machine takes the twenty, kicks out change in quarters, jackpot, scoop up all the quarters, shove them in my pockets, hands moving fast, almost forget the ticket dangling in my face. Grab the ticket, go back to the door, quarters jangling on both sides. Young man in a T-shirt stands between two ropes and tears tickets, logo of the theater across his chest, sends me off to the right, the Pocket Cinema screen, he says, theater B59. A sign hanging overhead from two wires says B59 and an arrow to the right, away from the theaters ahead of me where people are entering. Must be the right way, sign says so, directions from the staff, but no entrance to B59 in view. Keep going, it's here somewhere, smell of old carpet overwhelms the smell of popcorn. Down the hallway, dead end, turn left, only way to go, woman at an information desk, fresh lipstick around her smile, takes a look at the ticket, directs me ahead. Onward, she says, her smile getting bigger. This hallway darker, poor lighting, lower ceiling, storefronts, variety of music coming from the different stores, chaos of sound. People going into stores, others coming out, carrying shopping bags, dragging their feet, no signs over the doorways of some stores. Fork in the road, right, left, or straight ahead? A woman steps out of a store, my mouth opens to ask her directions just as someone inside the store calls her name and she goes back in. Increasing darkness ahead, dead end to the left, right seems best, but nothing that says B59 appears. No suite numbers on the doors, have a little faith, look for people with popcorn and cups with plastic covers and straws poking out of them. Another intersection comes up, four directions to choose from, including reversing course. To the right a wall that blocks passage, a closed door in the middle of it, young people huddled in front of the wall and up both sides, chatting, some wearing earphones. To the left more shops down a narrower hallway, stay straight, more light, more people, eye out for B59, still holding my ticket stub. Guy in a uniform, security guard maybe, two-way radio in hand, go toward him, he looks at the ticket stub, shakes his head, asks somebody on the other end of his radio if the name of the theater sounds familiar, no, never heard of it. Press on, eyes wide open, getting more crowded, entering an open area, a mall, high ceiling, stairs and escalators down, food court. Someone at a distance looks familiar, his face catches my eye through a group of people. He's moving away from me, go toward the face, a connection to something, someone to talk to, someone who might know something about which way to head, hard to find my way back without directions, orientation needed, sweat in my hairline, prickly sensation in my legs and chest. The head appears again in a gap between the shoppers, not getting any nearer, wondering who it is, then it hits me, but it can't be my father, dead for almost thirty years, before my ninth birthday, distant memory of his face, the man is too young, too tall, no reason to stay on the trail of a stranger, give it up, get help, go in a store, a jewelry store right here, a man wearing a tie stands behind a glass display case, show him the ticket stub. He blows air out of his mouth, stretches his left arm out to the left. Way back that way, he says, a maze, couldn't even draw you a picture. Thank him, take the stub, put it in my pocket, forget the movie, too late for it, try to retrace, go back by the same route, some sense of familiarity at first, but soon unsure which way to go, wandering into cul-de-sacs, give up on the idea of finding my way back, return to the mall and look for an exit to the street. The noise ahead leads me, the mall appears, walk straight to the end of a finger in the mall that will lead me outside, weave through the people, glass doors ahead. Relieved to grip the door handle, dark outside now, what's next, back to the hotel or back to the theater for a refund? Back to the theater, don't waste the money, they should hear that their signs are inadequate, which way, right or left, what's the difference? Right turn, chosen at random, keep moving, walk around the block if that's what it takes, another right at the corner, familiar street, same long block as before, is it worth it? A cab passes, moment of weakness, hail the cab, it screeches to a halt, run to the window, tell him the name of the hotel. No way, he says, already rolling, not worth my time, you can walk it, and he speeds away. Self-service is my comment to the back of his cab, the sound of his engine drowning me out. But better not to pay the cab and lose the price of the ticket, get a grip, continue down the long block, narrowing shadows in the distance, good place to get robbed, walk faster, coins weighing me down, making racket. Chest tightening as a gust of wind slams into me and knocks me back, corner must be where it was before, repeat it to myself, no point in going back, sooner the better, speed up the pace. Stomach roaring with hunger, socks stuck to the bottoms of my feet, reach the corner, take the turn, there it is, pull the door open, man with the blazer and tie still standing inside, same spot, sees me coming toward him. Take the ticket stub from my pocket, show it to him, tell him my story. Sorry, sorry, he says, we canceled the movie, our Pocket Cinema feature, locked the door, removed the easel and sign from the hallway, unusual, disappointing, not enough tickets sold to make it feasible to run, less than a handful of you, thought we caught everybody, strange filmmaker, lived alone in a cave for a year. What about putting up some better signs, what about a refund? He takes a special hole puncher from his pocket, holds the edge of my ticket, hole puncher leaves a pattern of tiny holes through it. Refunds are self-service, he says, around the corner where you bought your ticket, refund button on the side of the machine, insert the ticket stub, machine reads the holes. What if it fails? Bring it back in for a second punch, he says. Nod at that, and another question comes to mind.

TABLE

We'd planned to have dinner with the Hardaways at a restaurant we'd never been to, a popular new fish place. They had been there a number of times already, enough to be considered regulars and to know which table to ask for, so they made the reservation for four at 6:30. We were looking forward to the evening, but Katherine, Mrs. Hardaway, sent us a message the day before saying they had to cancel. She suddenly needed to have dental surgery and wouldn't be in any shape to enjoy the dinner.

Court and I decided we'd still like to go, and he called the restaurant to see if the Hardaways had canceled their reservation. They had not. Court told the person the Hardaways wouldn't be there and asked to change the reservation to our name and to move the time up to 6. We felt lucky to keep the table.

We got there at 6 on the button, a parking space near the door opened up, we pulled in, and Court joked that he'd phoned ahead to make sure a spot would be cleared for us. The host found our name on her screen, tapped the screen with her finger and we were off. The table was in a corner toward the back, an aquarium behind it, somewhat protected from foot traffic, the restaurant already filling up. Our waiter stopped by, introduced himself as Hugo, and took our drink orders, a martini for me and a beer for Court. We began scanning the menu, sharing ideas for a side dish we could split. The restaurant smelled appetizing, and Court commented, as he sometimes did when it applied, that the customers looked clean.

Soon Hugo served our drinks and we told him we wanted to enjoy them for a while before we ordered. No rush at all, he assured us. We took our time, and when we were ready we returned to the menu to make our selections.

We'd just told Hugo our order when I saw the Hardaways all the way up the aisle, past the bar, speaking with the host who'd seated us, another couple standing near them.

"Is it 6:30?" I asked Court.

"It is. Why do you ask?"

"Don't turn around, but the Hardaways are here and they have our stand-ins with them."

I gave Katherine and Jack a wave. Katherine nodded and Jack lifted his index finger an inch or so to acknowledge me.

"They're coming," I said, "and they're not bringing their friends with them."

"Holy crap. I wish we had bread so I could stuff my mouth full and point at it."

"We shouldn't be embarrassed. They're the ones who should explain."

"Looks like you made it," Jack said, forcing a sly grin and shaking Court's hand.

"I'm glad you're feeling better, Katherine," I said. I couldn't tell that she was in any pain.

"My doctor had a more urgent case come up at the last minute."

"Looks like we got your table," Court said, echoing Jack's attempt at an icebreaker.

The Hardaways didn't answer, and the way they looked at us annoyed me, as if the table should have been theirs. We didn't offer to yield to them.

"Sorry about the misunderstanding," Jack said. "We have friends waiting for us at the bar. The restaurant says they'll work us in."

They waved faintly and left, joining their friends, offering them an explanation, the couple quickly eyeing us. Court had his back to them but saw me watching.

"I sense we're being spoken of."

"I think so. By them and their friends who outrank us."

"I wonder what story they could be telling them," Court said. "Did you think Jack's jaw seemed a little tense?"

"Yes, and Katherine had that agitated undercurrent we've seen get into her before. I imagined her pulse pounding in her head."

"I don't feel like I belong at this table."

"That's how they want you to feel. I don't see where they get the right to claim it."

"They didn't cancel their reservation. I did."

"You think we should give it up?"

"No way. Though I do have mixed feelings."

So we had a subject that would stay with us as we drove home and brushed our teeth and tucked ourselves in bed.

Our food arrived promptly. We both loved our dishes, and Court gave his halibut a few defiant, celebratory smacks. The noise in the restaurant had steadily grown to a roar, and we had to raise our voices to hear ourselves. People were angling sideways in the aisle and the staff rushed around, altering course to avert collisions. As we ate, a woman waiting to be seated trolled the tables to see if anyone was close to finishing.

"Are they still at the bar?" Court asked.

"They are. The host is speaking with Jack. He's nodding. The aggressive customer who buzzed by sees them and is getting in the middle of it. The host is leaving them."

The table troller came our way, glancing over her shoulder at the Hardaways.

"I'm not going anywhere," I heard her say loudly.

Court heard her too. "If she asks if we're getting dessert, I say we refuse to cough up an answer."

The host approached the Hardaways again, menus in hand, and seated them and their friends at a table across from the bar. The troller noticed and rushed toward them, calling out that she was here first. She stood at their table and protested, the Hardaways ignoring her.

"How is everything?" Hugo appeared and startled us by asking.

"Dramatic," Court said.

Hugo nodded, unsure how to reply, and moved on.

"We have to pass them when we leave," I said.

"You could tell Katherine you'll call her tomorrow to see how she's doing."

"It'll be interesting to see if their friends know what I'm talking about."

"Or we could just act nice and smile."

"We'd regret it later if we did."

"We'd stay awake thinking of different things we should have said," Court agreed.

"We'd have only ourselves to blame. But if we're rude we'll look bad."

"You tell Katherine you'll call her. I could say we loved our table."

"Don't lay it on heavy. No sharp edges."

"What do you think they'll say?"

"Out loud, nothing. They want us out of here."

SYNC

I'd been out of sync with my surroundings for decades and considered it my natural state. I didn't know if I'd wandered off at a young age or if I'd been born out of sync and without a nose for the well-trodden path.

I was at an art gallery featuring an exhibition of historical black-and-white photographs, gazing at a picture of an older couple in worn and faded clothing standing in dirt in front of their unpainted porch, both of them utterly free of any desire to strike a pose that would cultivate a favorable impression of them. The woman wore an entrenched scowl that seemed to have nothing to do with the event of having her picture taken. The man, who was shoeless, yielded no facial expression and appeared to view the photographer's presence as irrelevant to him. I searched for something of myself in their aspect, but I remained separate from them, just as I felt separate from the various people at the gallery, some of them gathered in small groups and conversing, others taking in the photos. My eyes were focused on the folds beneath the scowling woman's eyes when I heard a familiar voice say my name.

The Benbrooks had been friends of mine, more or less, when I'd been married, though after Violet and I split they chose to remain friends with her instead of me. They made the right choice. It was Ben Benbrook who walked up to me, his gleaming row of dental veneers on display. The Benbrooks were exactly the type of people who put me on edge. They seemed desirous of drawing people out with their facade of contrived harmonic vibrations. Their constant air of ease made my skin crawl, chuckling and smiling at nothing, oblivious to anything miserable around them, blazing a trail of good cheer wherever they went. I could hardly keep myself from popping off at Benbrook whenever I spoke with him. He seemed to greet you happily for the sole purpose of embarrassing you for not being as happy and relaxed as he was. What did he want from you when he shook your hand? Did he want you to show your happy teeth and embrace him, try to outdo him with your merriment, flaunting how relaxing it was to see him?

Gary, Gary, Gary, he said, slapping me on the back with one hand and giving me a handshake with the other while flashing his veneers. He had a habit of repeating my name as if in disbelief. How long has it been? he asked. Still a bundle of futile and pointless nerves, I see. Ever ask yourself what the proper relation to things is and who you really want to be?

I've always wanted to ask you the same thing, I answered, seeing no reason to hold back.

He was laughing off my reply as Brenda Benbrook, his wife, came toward us. At the sight of me the flesh around her Botox injections sagged a notch. Gary, she said, with a look of horror. Hope you're well. She hurried off to a nearby gathering of people. So good to *see* you, I heard her sing to someone.

Rather than prolong the awkwardness, I told Benbrook I was sure he hadn't changed either, and then walked away.

You know, Gary, he said, gripping my retreating shoulder, I've been meaning to call you. We should get together for a drink sometime. Catch up on things.

A momentary downward turn of his facial muscles intrigued me, though they recovered quickly and assumed their mirthful position. Could someone else be lurking somewhere inside Benbrook? I agreed to meet him the next evening in the bar of a restaurant where the four of us used to go to dinner.

It was obvious as I sat at the table to join him that Benbrook had something on his mind, and he waited for our martinis to be served so he wouldn't be interrupted. His mouth twitched as if reluctant to translate his thoughts into words, and his eyes avoided mine when he spoke.

So you have to be wondering, he began, sighing. It's hard for me to tell you this, but I'm in love with Violet. I don't know how to talk about this subject with anyone and that's why I'm talking to you. I hope that didn't sound insulting, forgive me, I just thought you're the one person I know who would understand. This goes against all my beliefs. Vi senses something, I can tell, but I haven't said anything and how could I? It doesn't fit anywhere, does it? But maybe you think it does. I'm not asking you to sort out my feelings, don't misunderstand. That's not why I asked you here. I want to ask you a favor.

He looked up at me then. Did he expect me to agree without knowing what the favor was?

I know you still talk to Vi occasionally. She speaks fondly of you, can you imagine? Again, I don't mean to be insulting, but she's quite a person. What I'm trying to get around to is I want you to call and ask her not to yield to my desires, and I want her to know I asked you to tell her that. I think she'd be more at ease around me if she knew I had no expectations of her and wanted to be denied. I can't put my feelings for her out into the open. It makes me almost nauseated to think of speaking to her this way.

I see nothing unusual about the way you feel, I said, and

I don't think you need to be upset. If you can't deal with acting on your desires, then don't. But why tell her about them and why ask me to speak for you? You say you can't put your feelings out in the open, but that's what you're asking me to do.

I don't need to be upset? What about Brenda? This is complicated. I've never been through this before, if you're wondering. I'm not an affair guy, okay? I thought you'd know how to talk with her and that's why I'm asking you.

Vi won't want to hear this. Can't you see that? And if you don't say anything, Brenda won't have to hear it either.

I can tell Vi's not interested in me and I'm making her uncomfortable. I can't believe you'd refuse to help me, and especially her.

You want me to deal with your dark side because you can't own up to it. When you asked about my proper relation to things you were already trying to manipulate me into helping you. Were you in the proper relation to me when you greeted me with those insulting questions?

You think we're all animals, but less real and therefore beneath them, and people who want order and harmony in their lives are engaged in a performance and denying essential truths about themselves. But I think there's nothing wrong with wanting to be a better and more gracious person. I wish you thought so, too.

I don't have a problem with your wanting to be a better person. But no matter what we do, we can only be so good inside, and something about the way you're feeling could be making you fear I'm right. If you were a Buddhist monk you'd have to meditate for hours every single day to get the most out of whatever goodness was inside you, and you ain't no monk.

I dropped a twenty on the table and left, and at that moment I thought that was the end of the matter. But I kept thinking of Benbrook and how I'd left him with my dismissive lesson and without expressing any compassion for his suffering, which I had to admit was real. For years I'd wanted to see more suffering out of him, but when faced with it I'd tossed him aside. Couldn't I extend myself out of some sense of kinship with him as a person burdened by confusion and disorder? Something in me resisted this line of thought and the contact with Benbrook, but was that because he'd disparaged me and I wanted to retaliate by leaving him unaided? I didn't tell him I'd call her, fearing that at the last moment, as Vi's phone rang, I'd feel my throat constrict and chicken out.

As soon as Vi heard it was me, she asked if I could guess

who'd just called her with a confession.

The Twin B, she told me, using our nickname for Ben Benbrook. And since we got off the phone I can't stop thinking of what his real teeth look like underneath the veneers. He said he's fallen in love with me and there's nothing he can do about it. He doesn't want me to think he hopes anything will happen, but if something does, if he gets drunk on martinis and bangs on my door in the middle of the night, I should send him away. If he calls me in a moment of weakness, I should hang up on him. He asked me to help him keep his promise to himself that nothing can come of his feelings.

What did you tell him?

I told him not to worry and hung up.

It's what he asked you to do.

In a way I wanted to talk more, to get my thoughts in order, but how could I know what his intentions were? Did *he* know what his intentions were? Why call and tell me not to let him talk about the thing he was talking to me about? It doesn't make sense. Maybe he wanted me to say I had feelings for him, that I'd fantasized us being together, but I had no hidden feelings to share. I can't bear to imagine how long he's been thinking of me this way. Can you believe him making me listen to this stuff?

How can I be with them now? It would be like I've got a secret from Brenda; but if I tell her I'd be causing trouble. Why are you calling, anyway?

This is not the first I've heard of the Twin B's feelings for you.

You're kidding. How long have you known? I didn't know he confided in you. Does he love you, too?

No, he doesn't love me. I ran into them at a gallery and he asked me to have a drink with him. We met yesterday and he made a clean breast of it. He asked me to tell you that if he weakens, he does not want you to act on his desires. I told him I wouldn't do it. He must have felt desperate.

You said no but changed your mind.

He asked me to help and I thought I'd try.

Did you see Brenda? Did she seem upset?

The sight of me alarmed her, but I thought that was just normal revulsion.

Do you think she knows?

I don't have any idea, and I doubt he's a reliable witness. He thought you knew or at least suspected.

I had inklings but chose to ignore them. I'm amazed you'd let him twist you into being his spokesperson. I can't forget that whenever we planned to get together with the Benbrooks you indulged yourself in imaginary arguments for days before, even more so than with our other friends, and after we met, the internal arguments continued and you'd tell me all about them, always adding your one-sided commentary. I spent most of these evenings fearing you were on the verge of an eruption. You never stopped thinking less of them for being too nice, even for being relaxed. You imagined provoking disorder with them just to make some point that you alone understood. Well now we've got disorder, and I'm telling you I don't like it.

I'm sorry I got myself in the middle of this.

I'm the one who's in the middle. And Brenda, though she may not know she is. I'm getting off the phone now. Goodbye.

Less than half an hour after talking with Vi, her remarks still on my mind, my phone rang. I saw that it was Benbrook, but I dreaded continuing our conversation and telling him I'd called Vi. I considered deleting his message without listening to it, but I thought of him alone and mired in his upheaval.

I spoke with Vi, he whispered into the recorder, clearly not in recovery mode. I didn't feel like myself. My voice couldn't surrender to the words I was saying. I know you said you wouldn't call her, but in case you're still thinking about it I thought I should tell you you don't need to, and if you spoke with her now she'd only feel more tangled in the mess. I'm pretty sure Brenda's beginning to sense something's up with me. If she asks why Vi won't see us anymore, how will I explain it to her? Everything's gotten out of joint. I know you understand and I think that's one reason I spoke with you. You think I should accept what I feel, I know. I can't do that and I can't tell Brenda, even if she asks me. But I don't think she will. Things are quiet around here, and I'm trying not to hear what's inside the silence. That's the way we prefer it, Gary. Remember not to say anything to Vi. I see now I shouldn't have involved either of you. It would have seemed less real if I hadn't.

DINNER

We're at dinner with another couple and I am under self-imposed pressure to remain silent, except to order my food, on the grounds that my point of view would be unwelcome. Before we left the house, my wife told me that the world does not eagerly await more of my wisecracks, and experience tells me she is completely justified in this assessment. The couple consists of an old friend we see occasionally and his new sweetheart, a so-called soul mate, or so they believe at this early stage in the agony-inducing sweetness of their relationship. I'm trying not to listen to them, maintaining an understated and frozen smile that I fear could be in danger of thawing as the warm evening progresses. We're seated at an outside table and the restaurant is overwhelmed with customers, service is slower than usual, and servers intermittently race past our table carrying plates of hot food inches over our heads. As we sip our red wine, the couple can't stop beaming at each other and fondling hands and forearms and elbows, her aroused fingers sometimes twirling the gray hair flowing from the top of his partially unbuttoned shirt. The imagery is enough to threaten my silence and I remind myself, while we wait for our salads, that I must withhold all forms of commentary or my attitude toward them will inevitably seep through the cracks between and beneath the words. I must not argue, must not disagree, must not unveil revealing looks, must temper my inner verbiage, must prevent its content from showing on my face, and if challenged or accused of anything I must not defend myself. Of special importance is that if technology is mentioned I must not let myself be triggered into a diatribe about the soul-sucking properties of smartphones, how more and more people march around like zombies with their phones held in front of them even when they're not in use and how others sleep with their phones, probably tucked between their upper thighs in anticipation of the next vibrating call. As I've been told again and again, no one wants to listen to my warped perspective on the spreading epidemic of smartphone worship or on some people's habit of continuously streaming photos of their travels to their huge TVs whenever they have company, with Andrea Bocelli singing passionately in the background as if he were present at every moment on their trips.

In fact, talking to myself on this subject can compromise the integrity of my smile so I should cease babbling inwardly for the good of everyone at the table. I've vowed to let as little air as possible in through my mouth, though breathing exclusively through my nose becomes tiresome. When my Caesar salad gets here I'll have an excuse to open my mouth and can inhale deeply without detection as the salad enters. If I'm spoken to during the meal, I'll point to my bulging jaws and chew dramatically and then hope that by the time I swallow the topic will have changed.

I've had some success in not hearing them and I've also begun to avert my eyes, but I shouldn't appear disengaged, which could arouse suspicion and lead to exposure. The word *sweetie* has been used a number of times, but I've managed to avoid taking in the words that surrounded it, though their rapturous body language is hard to ignore.

I look around for an approaching server and sure enough here come our salads, what a relief. I calm down a bit, knowing I can now breathe more easily. Don't rush, chew slowly, extend the rest period. Despite my efforts to contain myself I begin to wonder if he's conscious of the density of her eyelash augmentation. Do her eyelids get fatigued heaving those things around all day? Does she attend eyelid exercise classes to develop their core muscles? And my devotion to chewing cannot completely distract me from the theme of self-admiration that runs through much of what they say. So thorough is their belief in their ability, as I hear them describe it, to bring together people and ideas to form a greater whole—

But stop, shut off the sound. Broaden the smile without overdoing it, don't draw their eyes in my direction. Make a cognitive adjustment, don't peek at the watch or seem ready for anything to conclude. Be here, look neutral. Don't say things that will later cause regret and hard feelings. Why relive the familiar pattern of wishing I hadn't come out with my thoughts and reproaching myself for offending people and then defending myself to myself and holding it against others for provoking me and for being offended, before circling back and reminding myself that I've let myself be provoked, that I am the instigator, a raving bore on the loose?

The server clears our plates, comments are made about the deliciousness of the salads, and our friend's chest hair absorbs another twirl. Water glasses are being refilled, and the server reappears and pours what's left of the wine. Our friend says he thinks we'd like another bottle. I pretend to be enjoying the night air, though sweat is dripping down my pant legs. I look around the patio and watch people speaking. I feel almost no connection with them and ask myself if they consider whether they feel connected to anyone around them. Each table seems to be its own territory, and I dread overhearing what any of them are saying and having to conceal my reaction to it. When we get home my wife may comment on the discussion at our table, and she may admit to a degree of frustration at not expressing herself, but she is far more comfortable in this situation than I am.

The new bottle of wine is presented and our glasses are topped off. I see that our friend's soul mate is looking directly at me, perhaps noting my failure to participate, and she asks how my work is going. I nod and look pleased and my wife picks up the answer from there, explaining that I don't like to talk about myself, the approach we agreed to earlier. I let my mind drift, hoping that my turn to speak will pass to someone else. My wife knows to change the subject, which she does, a book she's reading, have they read it?

Years and years have gone by and I'm still unsafe without a leash, my mouth a potential concern to anyone within its range. This line of thinking serves its purpose, keeps me under control, but it increases my sense of suppression and familiar questions occur to me about why I must hide my thoughts from others. I suffer momentary energy sags in my self-restraint and during one of these sags I hear him start to explain his choice of career, and before I know it I'm on the perilous course of listening to what he's saying.

He was in college, a young man with many ambitions, when a professor of his called him into his office. Of course, I was a gifted student, our friend off-handedly remarks, but the professor counseled him that he'd have to decide on only one career path, because as talented as he was and with so many viable options to choose from, he could not serve more than one master. Our friend says that this was the wisest advice he has ever been given, and his new sweetheart builds upon the narrative by saying that his talents in other areas remain undiminished. He fondles her elbow at this comment and lowers his head briefly to convince us of his fundamental humility.

The main courses arrive, deflecting my impulse to toast his enduring greatness, and the wine and water glasses are again replenished. I put my arm under the table and look at my watch, and a period of relative quiet ensues as we eat our food. I keep my head down, and when the talk resumes I hear her compliment the gifted student's ability to bond with people. He leans toward her and kisses her on the lips, and she makes a satisfied sound that suggests the kiss is tastier than her dinner. We are fortunate to be in their presence, this couple born to enrich the lives of others. I could no doubt learn much from them if I weren't completely incurable. Why do I not see in them what they see in themselves? Does the fault lie with me? Do I belong to the same race as this couple?

Sweat oozes out of me, my legs soaked with it. My chest hurts, food is sticking in my throat, but I'm determined not to say a word about my fear of choking. If I lose consciousness it will almost be worth it to escape being with these insufferable people. Where do they get the nerve to be so full of shit? Has anyone ever asked them this? Would it do them any good if I did? What would it accomplish, keep chewing and swallow gradually, drink some water and take it easy.

The water helps cool me down, but he sees the sweat on my face and asks if I'm okay. I nod, don't worry about me I imply. I wonder what I would have said if I'd said anything, but why imagine comments I'm not going to make, especially after the moment has passed? Do I want to agitate myself? The answer should be no; would that be true? Gifted student, indeed, and with a needy world all around him waiting to be awakened by his guiding light.

I tell myself the statement is too harsh, and just then she advises us to look up his social-media account. He likes to add statements of insight and wisdom onto it, he says, to help him connect with people and, he hopes, heighten their level of awareness. He has many followers, his sweetheart claims. Should I press the palms of my hands together and bow at his feet? Is that what's called for? Could it possibly help me?

A man asks if he should take my empty plate, and I again nod, stifling a belch and then another and another. He removes the other plates, and I reach down and pull up my socks, faintly chuckling to myself at the symbolism of this gesture and at the nature of their sock-shriveling conversation. I'm exhausted by my self-control, brain sinking gradually into mush, overwhelmed by the grandeur of the fabulous couple, who are engaged in advanced beaming and fondling now that their plates are no longer in their way. Where do these people come from? How do they sustain the intoxicated pitch of their self-aggrandizement? Do they believe it themselves?

Eventually the server brings the check and puts it next to our friend, who insists on paying. My wife protests, but I hold to the rule of limiting passage through my body's largest orifice. In less than a minute the server returns with the credit card and receipt, and the gifted student quickly calculates the tip and squiggles his name. They both let us know they've got meetings scheduled for early in the morning, and they share a contented laugh at how full their calendars are and how that never seems to change, but they, of course, love the active pace and reaching out to people. We are all one person really, she tells us.

We walk to our cars and exchange hugs, she exclaiming how much she enjoyed meeting us, he letting out a practiced groan of pleasure as he clutches my wife and gives her parallel air kisses. He slaps me on the back several times after releasing me, sharing his positive energy, lucky man that I am, a fortifying boost of superiority to carry with me. I push the button on my key fob to unlock our car and we get in.

Whewwww, my wife says and caresses the back of my head as we roll slowly away from them.

GETAWAY

Van had planned a getaway to a place where he knew no one and could be left in peace, the only drawback being that his mind would travel with him. Many times he'd told himself never to express an opinion again, and whenever possible not to speak. He carried a pen and pad, and when someone addressed him directly, he'd reply by scribbling a note. In traffic he'd sometimes blurt out a curse or mutter in a way that disturbed him, memories of past muttering coming back to haunt him. He'd tell himself to shut up, without saying it out loud, because he couldn't stand the sound of his own voice. His notes at times failed to conceal his true nature, and few people could endure with patience his handwritten monologues. He saw himself as unfit for human society, and he could not recall any good he'd ever accomplished by opening his mouth to speak. Communication simply didn't work for him.

As he pretended to read the screen on his smartphone, someone approached him and leaned toward his chair in the gate area for his flight. He'd known the leaning man as a boy in the suburban neighborhood where they'd grown up, recognized him at once through the added weight and gray hair.

Excuse me, Les said, are you Van?

He wondered if he should admit being who he was, if he should reply at all, and if they would be seated near each other on the plane. He hadn't seen Les in decades and Les might invite him to dinner to share life stories. Rather than pull out his pad and write Les a note, Van shook his head.

Les stood straight up and offered a handshake, saying his first and last names. Van couldn't leave Les's hand hanging between them, so he shook it. He rejected the idea of making up a name, and his voice could strike Les as familiar. He saw no one standing near Les, though his wife or other traveling companion could be in the restroom and could appear at his side and ask to be brought up to date. Van would have to sit quietly as Les explained who the man in the chair might or might not be. Les didn't glance behind him to see if a companion could be approaching, but he leaned closer than before and said that he knew who he was talking to and he didn't like being disrespected and couldn't understand it. He then left Van and sat in a chair by the wall.

The time passed slowly and Van heard Les clearing his throat and coughing several times, possibly a ploy to get Van to turn and look. Les could at any moment make another run at him, putting his mouth to Van's ear. Van googled Les and pictured Les googling him. He knew of several images Les could have found that proved he was lying, but Les did not bring his phone over and confront him with his own image.

Van kept his head down as they boarded the plane and did not see where Les sat, though he took a peek to see if he was nearby. He worried that his behavior at the airport might cause retaliation that would ruin his getaway. He tried to sleep and forget during the flight, resisting his fear that Les might tap him on the shoulder and insist on an explanation and an apology.

He saw nothing of Les while in the air or after landing, and he hopped in a taxi that took him to the beach resort he'd booked for several days. The odds were long that Les would be staying there, but he scanned the lobby and the restaurant at dinner for any sign of him and prepared himself to make a sudden exit. As far as he could tell the resort was free of Les, and he imagined himself on the beach the next day with a margarita and his Paul Bowles novel drowning out any thoughts that would have originated with him.

Before he could get out the door the next morning the phone in his room rang. Who could it be, no one knew where he was, if he picked it up he'd have to answer. After the ringing stopped, he waited a moment and checked to see if the caller had left a message. There was none, and he sat on the bed, his mind running. Les could have called the larger resorts on the beach until he found him and asked to be put through to his room. Van wished he could tell Les that if he got him talking he'd end up wishing he hadn't, but he cut off this line of thought; obsessing about Les would ruin his trip. The call could have come from someone working for the hotel, and Les had likely forgotten about him by now and could be having a rollicking time with friends.

Van dressed for breakfast and took the elevator down. When the door opened he started across the lobby and saw Les rising from a chair and coming toward him. He saw no point in trying to flee or resist. Les stopped in front of him and raised his hands, his manner suggesting he'd like to have his say. Van looked into his eyes. Les didn't expect Van to speak, he said; he wanted a listener, someone to talk to about his failed life, and someone he'd known but wouldn't see again would be perfect. Think about it, Les said, and if Van decided it was okay, they could meet here for dinner. No pressure, no need to reciprocate with an account of his life, just listening, and after dinner, he vowed, they'd go their own ways.

Intrigued, Van watched Les walk away. If he could read a novel, why couldn't he listen to another person's story? He ate his chilaquiles and adjusted himself to the proposal. Would he be tempted to speak? He could communicate with his face or gestures or give Les a slap on the back if the situation called for it. He spent the day on the beach with his novel, slowly sipping a margarita, determined that he could meet Les without thinking how it would affect him.

He came down on the elevator at half past six and saw Les getting up from the same chair. It was a clear and calm evening and they sat at a table on the patio, Les declaring that the dinner was on him and ordering margaritas for both of them. He didn't mention Van's reticence at the airport or comment or furrow his brow when Van ordered using his pen and pad. At first he spoke generally about never knowing what he was doing or why he did things, beyond working to make enough money to pay his bills and support his family. Always he suspected himself of having selfish intentions and lacking goodwill toward others. He tended to mouth off to his bosses, for example, and shout at people who bothered him and then rationalize that he felt a strong impulse to be honest in expressing himself, which was nonsense, since he well knew that he lied to himself and others and had never shown a serious interest in truth or justice. He'd been married twice, both times to women who suffered from addictions, one to prescription drugs and the other to alcohol. He liked to drink with both of them and up to a point he enjoyed acting crazy with them, arguing with whatever they happened to be watching on television and shouting at their so-called friends, most often when they were alone in the house and their friends could not hear them. These bouts of shouting led to them shouting at each other, and his kids, one from each marriage, grew up shouting. They'd both run off and struggled for years to stay employed, his son now locked up in prison for robbing people's houses, his daughter residing in some unrevealed location to keep him the hell away from her. He believed he'd wanted them for the dubious purpose of perpetuating himself, he said, and he regretted putting them in that position. His first ex-wife died from what he called unintentional suicide and he'd lost track of his second ex, who'd been fond of telling him that he needed to add an *s* to the end of his first name. Les confessed that he'd enabled his wives by behaving in much the same way they did, until they couldn't take the sight and sound of him any longer. He'd flunked out of AA, he told Van, clutching the stem of his margarita glass, and one idea that constantly haunted him was that he was the source of all his troubles. He injected the poison between himself and those he encountered, his voice a scourge that had dragged him around by the mouth and tongue throughout his life. His stupidity and misguidedness reached deeper than his conscious awareness, and the devastating truth, according to Les, was that he must have wanted to do everything he had done, and if he had it to do over, he'd probably make the same mistakes again. What excuse could he offer for himself? he asked Van rhetorically as they were served their dinners. His worst enemy was himself, he continued, and he was always there, following himself around, insisting on his way, as if serving a Greater Les, an absurd phrase he'd coined and repeated to himself in self-deprecation for many years. He had never told his story, if it could be called that, to anyone, he said, and the longer he lived the more it burdened him. He had no illusion of cleansing himself by his admissions, and he hoped he wasn't leaving the impression that he sought advice or some remedy. A long silence ensued, and Les then apologized for intruding on Van's trip. Isn't this beef terrible? he said, and Van nodded.

Van's mind churned through words he could say, stirred by how much he and Les had in common. He remained silent but clasped his hands and jabbed his thumbs at his chest as he looked across the table at Les. Les eyed Van and their empty glasses and waved at the server. Van turned his glass upside down. Les ordered himself another drink.

FROM

Gina called to say that my older brother was living in a memory-care facility. His daughter had told her about it. Gina had been to visit him and she thought I'd want to hear how much he'd changed. He won't know you, she said. I wondered how she'd made out with him. She'd always struggled to make ends meet, and it was sort of a hobby with her to talk men out of their money. She asked if I knew if he'd ever written up a will. I said I had no idea, though if he had he'd probably left everything to himself. She said it surprised her more people didn't do that.

I thought it over, questioning the purity of my motives, but decided to go see him anyway. I hadn't laid eyes on him in twenty years. We'd had a falling out, many of them actually, starting when I grew to be as big as he was. When I was little, he had the strength to dominate me. He'd throw me out of the house before our mother came home from work and lock all the doors so I couldn't get back in. Sometimes if I stood close to his window I could hear him groaning inside. But who wants to know the details?

I found him in a common room sitting at a table next to

a woman with a startled look, her short hair almost upright. My brother sat with his mouth slightly open, his eyes seeming to float in some unknown fluid inside his head. I stood in front of him until he looked at me. I moved closer and said my name.

"I'm your brother," I said. "I'm here for a visit."

"Really? That's wonderful! A visitor. Please join us."

I sat opposite him, the woman to my right. Had I wanted to see him this way? Had I been waiting?

"Introduce yourself," he said to the woman.

"I'm Betsy."

"My brother, you say. How old did you say I am?"

"I didn't. You're 82. I'm 73."

"You're just a young fella."

My brother turned in his chair and addressed a few people slumped on couches.

"Hear that, a visitor's come to see me. Isn't that wonderful!"

Two of them looked up at the sound of his voice.

"Where are you from, Betsy?" I asked.

She paused. "I don't remember," she said.

"It's good to meet you. Is my brother treating you all right?"

She nodded.

A friendly staff member appeared at the table.

"How's everything going here?" he asked, his hand on my brother's back.

"This is my visitor. Why don't you tell him your name?"

"Dwyatt," he said and shook my hand. "Just let us know if there's anything we can do." He waved and departed.

"Someone named him that," my brother said, "maybe his mother." He peeked over his shoulder to see if Dwyatt could hear him.

"I've got a nice room," he said then. "Would you like to see it?" He stood and pointed.

I said goodbye to Betsy and followed him, hearing him puff on the way. He entered a spacious room with a small dresser, a chair, and a little table next to the bed. He went straight to the bed and sat on top of it, smiling, and asked me to take a seat in the chair.

"Nice of you to visit. I wanted you to meet someone."

He gestured toward a doll on the tabletop, her back propped against the wall. She wore a red dress, a blond wig, and a little hat.

"This is Gina. She's my girlfriend."

I tried not to react. I hadn't seen Gina's mother in a long time, except once when I happened to walk right past her at a shopping mall. She didn't seem to recognize me. Gina looked a little bit like me, but so did my brother, and I'd always wondered if he could be her real father.

"Gina's my daughter's name. She visited you, not long ago."

"Well," he said, eyeing the doll, "I can tell she wants to take her clothes off. But I haven't kissed her yet."

A memory came up then, the time of our last falling out. He claimed he wanted me to explain my paintings, but that wasn't what he really wanted.

"There's nothing I can identify in them," he said. "They look like a small child could have painted them. They look like the side of my garage."

"Identify?" I said. "You sure you know what that means?"

He resented my tone, as he always did when he thought I challenged his rank in the birth order.

"I'm still your big brother," he told me, puffing himself up. "Nothing can change that."

"Not yet," I said.

SHIRL

People stick to you inside and you can't get them out, and the more you try the more whatever of them is inside you fights back. Shirl, for example, a woman I work closely with. Her voice won't leave me alone, even staying with me during the night. She gets mad at me because I don't want to hear her family's problems. If she tells me her grown-up children are addicted or otherwise troubled, I don't have advice or a solution. It's up to her to decide how much she can take from her husband and how to deal with her crazy sister calling her up with her worries when she can't sleep. I turn away from the details, which hurts her feelings. She wants a girlfriend to confide in, and I won't cooperate.

After a night of drinking several glasses of wine that failed to drown her out, I went to work with a headache, determined to silence her if she started the morning with some horrible new tale. I put my things in my locker and took my usual path to the sorting area, where at once I heard people talking about her. Her son, Leo, had been killed. Around midnight he'd broken

123

into an apartment looking for a woman who'd been hiding from him, and an armed man had rushed out of a hallway inside and shot him in the chest. Shirl's husband became unruly when the police couldn't answer his questions about the shooting and had to be restrained by more than one officer. Watching them, Shirl collapsed and lost consciousness. She had been confined to a hospital bed.

I contributed to the collection the staff took up for her family, and I thought all day of visiting her, urging myself to do it no matter how uncomfortable it made me. I imagined her weeping and clutching me in a suffocating embrace.

Later, I drove up the ramp into the hospital's parking garage and found a space with no cars on either side. But the thought of having to hear what she'd endured froze me. I didn't want to stand at her bedside and hold her hand. If I touched her, something would change between us.

She stayed with me on the way home and as I sat drinking my wine. I woke the next morning thinking of her.

HOTEL ROOM

I'd arrived for a job interview. My hotel was located in a small town near the large town where the interview was scheduled. The room had no TV, no phone, and no clock. The hotel had no elevator, and my room was two flights up a spiral staircase. I knew when I booked the room that I'd have no TV, phone, clock, or elevator but I booked it anyway and at my own expense. I spent the afternoon sitting up in bed wanting as little on my mind as possible, glad not to have TV noise interfering with the quiet.

I'd stayed in this room, or one exactly like it, with my wife the year before, a weekend I enjoyed much more than she did. I had memories of looking out the windows along one side of the room at a square that had little foot traffic. Only two stores were open on the square and on occasion a customer or a cat would walk by. I liked watching the slow developments taking place outside the window. My wife might have been interested if she'd looked, but she didn't think it was worth her time.

The hotel wasn't the most convenient place I could have chosen, but it was only a twenty-minute drive to the interview and I could clear my head and enjoy the familiarity. As far as I could tell there were only two other parties staying at the hotel and that added to my sense of calm, though my calm was fragile and shallow, as if I couldn't quite make out whispered words or roiling images beneath it.

My interview was mid-morning the next day and I hadn't been able to imagine myself there. I had no mental image of the building where it would take place and no image of the body that went with the voice that had spoken with me on the phone. I'd been through many interviews, but not in years, and I hadn't thought of a single question they might ask me and hadn't made any plan how to present myself.

The common rooms at the hotel were darker than I remembered, perhaps because they were trying to save on electricity. At dinner I had the option of sitting in the dining room or outside on the patio. The weather was what anyone would call wonderful, perfect temperature and no wind, but on the previous visit we'd eaten outside and flies had soared at us and at our food. I decided to escape fly harassment this time and eat in the dining room.

Almost no lights were on in the dining room, but the sun had not set and I sat at a window with a view of the empty square. The owner of the hotel did the cooking and she took pleasure in preparing dishes for her guests. The other parties had not yet come down, and I enjoyed the stillness before they appeared. But it wasn't long until I heard the first group and then the second coming down the staircase, all of them looking as if they'd had a shower within the last thirty minutes, their skin gleaming, their clothes fresh. Both groups chose to eat on the patio. I couldn't see the patio from the dining room, but I could soon hear the sound of talking and laughter. I felt some curiosity, but I didn't ask the owner to move me outside. They'd know I'd moved from the dining room and assume I hoped to be part of the merriment. They could all know one another and I could be seen as an interloper. Besides, I wanted solitude.

I ate the veal kidneys that night. They were crunchy and delicious, just as they'd been on my earlier stay at the hotel. Quiet reigned on the square, and aside from the patio the only distraction was that I noticed a small door, slightly ajar, in the wall ahead of me. I wondered what was behind the door and imagined crawling through the opening to see what was inside and how far it extended.

After eating I returned to my room and took in the view of the square. Only fleetingly did my mind turn to the job interview. I couldn't get a handle on what to think of it and I put off any consideration of the interview until morning. I was somewhat distracted thinking how unhappy my wife would have been with me, but being alone I was satisfied enough looking out the window and settling down.

In the morning I went down to breakfast, which was included in the price of the room, and ate everything put in front of me before the other guests made it down the stairs. About the time I finished eating it occurred to me that I hadn't considered what route I'd take to the interview and that if I was going I'd have to leave in less than two hours. As I climbed the winding stairs on the way back to my room, a mounting pressure began to squeeze me. I was beginning to realize that I had no intention of going to the interview. I had nothing to say to those people. I'd been on teams that had interviewed candidates with nothing to say and who looked miserable every second, and after those candidates left the room everyone on the team wondered out loud why they'd shown up. I was merely asking myself this same question in advance. So I made up my mind I wasn't going.

But the consequences of my decision weighed on me. I didn't call the company and tell them, and I wondered if they would call the hotel. I'd told them where I was staying. And what would I say to my wife? Whatever I said I couldn't imagine she'd be sympathetic, and why should she be? What sort of half-baked person was she living with? The only explanation I could think of was that I'd changed my mind about wanting the job. I'd never wanted it, but everyone didn't have to know that.

I was glad I'd planned to be at the hotel another night. I could take a walk in the town and try to get my thoughts in some kind of order. I remembered walking its streets and being struck by how few people I saw. My wife found the empty streets eerie. In two cases we noticed sets of keys sticking out of front doors.

About an hour after the scheduled interview time someone from the company called the hotel. A short man with a long beard came up the staircase and knocked on my door. I'd seen him around the hotel, sometimes with a cat following him. I had no idea what to say when he told me the man was holding for me on the phone. I was on my way out for a walk, but I couldn't see that as an excuse not to take the call. The problem was I had no excuse. I asked him to say that I couldn't come to the phone. Should I take a message? he asked. If he offers to leave one, yes. Thank you, I said and closed the door. I stood holding the knob, wondering why I'd put myself in such an untenable position.

I waited several minutes and then rushed down the stairs

and out the dining-room door for my walk, hoping the bearded man wouldn't see me and deliver a message.

The town was just as I remembered it. I saw remarkably few businesses anywhere around and only a handful of people getting some air. There were scattered parked cars, but I didn't see anyone driving. I stood for some time on a street corner that I'd remembered and, as before, looked in every direction without seeing anything moving. I could feel myself breathing, and I asked myself why I'd want to be at the job interview when I could be here.

The moment I stepped inside the dining-room door I heard voices at the front desk. A man from the company was asking about me, mild concern in his voice. The front desk was around the corner and they hadn't seen me. Their discussion would have to lead to a trip upstairs to knock on my door. If I went back out they might hear me so I hurried on tiptoe to the small door in the wall and swung it open. There was crawl space inside, and I scooted into it and pulled the door almost shut, thinking that if it closed it might lock, which would leave me in the predicament of knocking on the door from the inside so I could get out. The space was tight and dark, and I'd have a hard time turning around. I felt along the wall and found a light switch and flipped it on for a second. I turned it off, thinking that a person passing through the dining room might catch sight of the dim light. I'd seen nothing ahead, but I heard distant voices talking over one another, in conflict. I guessed the voices could be coming from hotel staff, yet for some reason they struck me as sounds of my own disorientation. The space had no airflow, and as far as I could tell it wasn't being used for storage. I was thinking it could lead somewhere, to a door outside or to a room. If I continued moving forward I might come to a larger space where I could turn my head back toward where I came in. Or I might not. I could hear the voices of the company man and the owner, who had gone upstairs already and failed to find me.

The company man said he'd wait awhile for me. Why had he come and why did he persist? I had nothing to tell this man. I'd have to stay put until he left, but I could only hear so much and I'd be lucky if I knew when that was.

My wife was hosting a party at our house. A girlfriend of hers was visiting from out of town and my wife had asked a number of their girlfriends over to celebrate. She'd made it plain she didn't want me at the party. I could either leave the house or show my face just long enough to say hello and then claim

I had work to do in my study. Anything less than a hello would seem rude, she said. She seemed disappointed when I said I'd spend the time in my study. No men were invited to the party so it wasn't that odd for me not to be included, but her dismissive tone rankled me.

Her attitude was consistent with the way she'd been acting around me. Tension showed in her face when I came near her, and she didn't reply spontaneously to anything I said and often went through a painstaking mental process before speaking. She didn't feel completely there when I held her and seemed to wish I'd let her go.

Soon after the festivities got going I did as instructed and said hello to her guests, making no conversation, not even small talk. I kept my head down and made a quick disappearance.

In my study I pulled out my notebook and wrote the narrative about going to the hotel room. Though I'd stayed at the hotel before, I hadn't gone there a second time and had no job interview in a nearby town. My wife had not enjoyed our stay.

When I reached the end I set my pen down and read what I'd written. Why schedule an interview for a job I didn't want? I had a job that bored me, but I wasn't looking for another one. Why had I put myself in the hotel room? Why did I still hear the muffled voices at the end of the crawl space? Why did I imagine myself on the street corner, closing my eyes, sealing myself in solitude?

I heard a guest calling my name from our den. I answered the call, glancing at my wife's face as I neared them. What are you doing back there? the guest asked. Writing a story, I said. Read it to us, she said. It would take too long, I answered and saw my wife nod at me. What's it about? I didn't answer that one. I waved at them and said I'd better get back to work before I lost my train of thought.

I returned to the street corner, and now it came to me that my mind had gone back there many times, looking around, seeing and hearing no one. The memory followed me back to the hotel room. I sat with my notebook, adding the second section to the story and reading the narrative through, the quiet square outside, only a cat moving, its soft steps soundless.

At the end I flipped the notebook shut, at that moment no one coming toward me or expecting me. I asked myself how long I could stay there and where I would go when I left.

INTRUDER

Hearing my neighbor's voice through our common wall fed my curiosity since I knew he could be addressing no one but himself. I put my ear to the wall but couldn't make out the words. At times I heard him curse in a somewhat louder voice, a limited outburst possibly brought on by the pressure of his extreme isolation. Could he be dangerous? Could he be plotting something I might later wish I'd known more about? Did he spend long hours viewing websites that fed an ever-expanding paranoia?

I wanted answers, and I came up with an idea. Due to our nearness, I became aware of some of his habits. He liked to stay in his apartment, but he had to buy provisions and he left every Tuesday at a certain time to tote his garbage down. I could see him through my peephole, walking to the elevator, trash bag in hand, and I imagined over and over that I'd go into his place after he left and hide myself somewhere. The aggressive aspect of it was unnerving, but I grew determined, despite fearing he'd discover me.

I chose a Tuesday and made preparations. I ate something, used the bathroom, put a small notebook and pen in my pocket, and stood at the peephole. When he came out, I watched him press the button for the elevator, his legs jittery and his lips moving until the elevator appeared. As soon as its door closed and the elevator started down I popped out and tried his door. He hadn't locked it since he'd only be gone for a few minutes, and I entered his apartment, hurrying to find a hiding place before he got back.

The entryway was lined with newspapers stacked as high as he could comfortably reach. I passed the bathroom and kitchen, and stuck my head into his bedroom on the left. Single bed, rumpled bedclothes, filing cabinets along the walls, cluttered bedside table. L-shaped desk in the living area, computer and printer, notebook open, handwriting slanted forty-five degrees to the left, more newspaper and rows of filing cabinets with belongings and years of notebooks jumbled on top, pages filled with words, shades down in every room, desk lamp on, the only light on in the apartment. To the right, mass of stacked newspapers, a corridor around the back with a nook in the middle for access. I came to rest in the nook, and within a minute he returned. I heard him go to the kitchen and wash his hands, talking to himself over the running water and as he walked into the living area and sat at his desk.

I didn't have to wait long before I heard him writing, his

voice rising out of him. "Not speaking leaves the words trapped inside, struggling against the will to suppress them, even during sleep." He paused and repeated the line, and I scribbled what he said in my pad. "Restraint depletes me. Words are often more notable for what they don't say than for what they do say." He continued to write, but he whispered the words and I couldn't hear them. After a while he got up and paced, talking under his breath in anger, raising his voice briefly when he cursed. At one point I thought he approached our common wall and let loose an outburst that lasted only seconds. Was he picturing me there? "I haven't uttered a word I shouldn't have," he said, his footsteps somehow coordinated with the cadence of his voice, "and in some ways I regret that." Did his words suggest a suppressed desire to do me harm?

I needed to adjust my position, and I stretched myself out. I heard his pacing stop and wondered if he'd heard me shift and if he would come toward me and unleash a tirade at the sight of me; but he returned to his desk and resumed his narrative or notes, repeating to himself in a low voice: "Veneer worn thin, veneer worn thin." A relatively quiet period followed, and eventually he left the room. I was tempted to crawl down the corridor and peek around a corner, but if I moved I risked discovery and what did I hope to see?

He soon came back to his desk and I heard him at the keyboard, exclaiming at what he read. "Idiots, human nature at its finest." An hour went by before I again heard him speak. "I couldn't remember that he'd ever laid eyes on me for a second, even when I tried to engage him in conversation. He had me pegged, I imagined, as a man concerned only with his own orbit." Could I have been the "I" in these lines? "I sat in the front window, rotating the warm cup in my hand, noticing heads sticking up in parked cars. I watched the faces of passersby, asking myself if any of them might know more about him than I did."

He wrote awhile longer, until he finally heaved a sigh and went to his kitchen. He opened cabinets and the refrigerator, groaning as he searched for something. He rushed out the door, I supposed for a missing ingredient.

I'd had enough and I needed to pee, but I wanted a look at his desk. I quickly flipped through his notebook, but his slanted handwriting was almost illegible and the fear of him returning distracted me. I put the notebook at the angle I'd found it and went through the corridor of newspapers to the door, using the thumbturn to unlock it. As I stepped through the doorway the neighbor on the other side of the elevator, a young woman with shoulder-length dark purple hair, opened her door and saw me, and her eyes fixed on my face. She hadn't lived in her place long and didn't know me, but she must have been thinking I did not belong in our neighbor's apartment and that she may have caught me in some illegal activity. I turned away from her, eager to put my door between us.

I went straight to the toilet and relieved myself, then washed my hands and arms and face. I was drinking water in the kitchen when I heard a knock. Checking the peephole, I saw the young woman looking toward our neighbor's apartment, the tattoo on the nape of her neck showing through her purple hair. I opened up.

"Well, well, well. The mysterious intruder."

She gazed at me, and my mind's eye scanned my apartment, bed made, kitchen not too bad, no noticeable odor, no one else had been inside for months, not used to viewing it through other people's eyes. I invited her in, thinking she expected it. I led her into the living area and she took a seat in a chair. I sat on the sofa, facing her. Her neck tattoo continued under her top, and I could only imagine how many others were covered by her clothing. I estimated that I was thirty years older than she was.

"So you have an interest in our neighbor."

"I've been curious about him."

"You broke in or walked in, am I right? That's intriguing." She watched me taking her in, the ease of her manner putting me on edge. "Would you like to pour me some wine? I drink red."

I hesitated but went to the kitchen, wondering what I could be letting myself in for. I imagined her getting to her feet and looking around the room. Would she find anything I didn't want her to see? I picked up a red wine with a twist top and opened it, grabbed two glasses and hurried back, catching my breath on the way. I found her seated, no air of movement about her. I set the glasses down and poured and handed her a glass. We both tasted the wine, and she clucked her tongue on the roof of her mouth.

"I think it's creepy you'd go in there. Why do you care what he does? When I go to bed at night, should I check under it to see if you're there?"

"Not necessary."

"Aren't you curious about me? Enough to mount another invasion?"

Why had I let her in? Did I think I deserved this?

"I'm a curious person too, and I feel torn between my curiosity and respecting his privacy. I have an uncle who lives alone and almost never comes out of his apartment. He surrounds himself with old newspapers and filing cabinets, and I hear he's reluctant to turn on a light. He doesn't even see relatives or talk to us on the phone or send us messages over the computer. He claims he has nothing to report, but we feel abandoned by him. He wouldn't recognize me anymore because he hasn't seen me since I was a little girl, but I still feel protective of him and worry about his isolation and vulnerability. My mother, my uncle's sister, told me a story about him. He wanted to meet with a lawyer, so he asked the lawyer to come to his apartment. When he arrived, my uncle opened the door to let him in and immediately turned his back. He told the lawyer to stand at the closed door until my uncle called out to him and then to walk between the stacks of newspapers to the back room. He should sit in the chair in front of the desk but face away from the desk and not ever look behind him. He followed my uncle's instructions, and after he'd seated himself in the chair my uncle rose from under the desk and sat and talked with the lawyer until he made up his mind to hire him. He told him they had an agreement, and the lawyer stood and walked straight ahead and out the front door without ever seeing my uncle and without my uncle seeing his face."

Her story hung in the silence. Was it true? Where would her mother have heard it? Her eyes stayed on me, perhaps tempting me to ask if our neighbor was her uncle, though if I asked she might laugh and deny it even if it was true. She refilled her wine glass and took a swallow.

"Do you have any feeling that you've violated his privacy?" she asked. "No answer? Then tell me, what does he do when he's alone? Did you learn anything that enriches your life or explains why he is the way he is? Did you experience the glow of conquest? Are you going to talk to me, or do you just want to look?"

She drank down the rest of her wine and stood and set the glass on the table beside me. She leaned down, her face close to my face, just above it, nearly touching, her hair on my cheek.

"You'd like to get a shower, wouldn't you?"

I guessed she'd sized me up before coming in, older than she was, slight build, wispy gray hair. She figured she was fit enough to take me if she needed to, and she could have a knife or some other weapon concealed on her somewhere. She moved closer, her mouth at my ear.

"Surprised you're so gutless, afraid to move or to speak. Are you going back in? Don't worry, I won't tell him. Better if it's our secret, don't you think? I'll see you inside your head, or wherever."

She walked out, but her aura remained. I took a sip of

wine, coughing as it went down. Despite what she'd said, I feared she'd rat me out and what they would do to me if she did. They could enter my place and tear it apart or torment me in ways I couldn't imagine. She'd enjoyed watching me squirm and might like to see more. Did she have an uncle? Did she want me thinking this way? Did she want me to go back in?

"Veneer worn thin," I muttered. "Veneer worn thin."

SURRENDER

He sits in his study, spiral notebook on his desk, pen resting on it, frozen gaze, nothing added to the page since yesterday. He appears besieged from inside. What is it? I ask. He looks at me but says nothing.

Next day, his notebooks are stacked on his desk. He's reading through them, a trace of searching in his eyes. He doesn't see me watching, and I leave him there alone with them. He's never wanted me to read his notebooks, his life's course chronicled in their pages. I don't want to force my way in, and I've seen it as good that he's been devoted to them, a way of making sense of things, of himself, I imagined, some foothold on his existence. But now?

Second day of reading the notebooks. I interrupt him.

How's it going? I ask.

He raises his head, his face telling me he wished I hadn't asked. He's never talked much, never felt at ease explaining or expressing himself. More comfortable with me than with others. Aloof, though not in an affected way. I go to his desk and kiss him.

Thank you, he says.

Anything I can do?

Nothing, he says. I'll keep reading.

I tell him I hope he finds it, and he smiles at me and then goes back to his spiral, an old one written decades ago.

He's put more work into the notebooks since he retired from public service. He'd never say he retired to devote more time to them, but I know he wanted to see where they would go. He must have had catching up to do and thoughts to add now that he has time to reflect on them. He'd always shown a tendency to become absorbed in the world in his head, people talking to him in there, arguments escalating, narratives unfolding. He couldn't live them all, couldn't let himself wander wherever his mind took him. In his notebooks he could release what was in his head, but he kept them to himself.

That night in bed, I make an effort to hold him. I embrace him almost the whole night. We change positions, but I keep my body against his. In the morning he kisses me. It helps, he says.

He gets up, goes through the paper during his bowl of cereal, then disappears into his study to read.

Nothing stirring for a couple of hours. I hesitate to go in there, not wanting to pressure him or to make him feel spied on. I want to see his face, estimate his thoughts as he assesses what he's written, his nature spilling out into a form he's taken some care with. From the kitchen I hear him turning a page now and then. I feel ridiculous standing at a distance listening to him, or listening to his silence. Does he sense that I'm there? Am I distracting him? I go to his door and he hears me and looks up.

I want to help, I say, and take a step toward his desk.

I don't know what you can do, he answers.

I can see he's not having a good day, the pages worrying him, an inkling of defeat on his brow. I nod, suspended in the silence.

I'm here anyway, I say. Let me know.

I appreciate it, he says.

The reading continues into the afternoon. A sigh comes from the study occasionally, and muttering. From the sound of it, my guess is that he's angry at himself.

At last he emerges, looking as if he doesn't know where he is. He knows he's in our house, but within himself, where is he and how did he get there? How did this happen? he seems to want to know. Have his spirals made him wonder? If I'm right he doesn't expect answers from me, and he doesn't want me staring at him, trying to read his mind. He says he has some books on hold at the library.

I need to read something else, he says and tries and fails to chuckle at himself.

He gets his keys and wallet and gives me a quick kiss, holding my hand tight for a moment before he leaves.

The following day I stick my head into his study and tell him I'm on my way out for lunch with a girlfriend. He doesn't appear to remember that I mentioned the lunch to him yesterday, but I know he's been distracted. I leave him occupied with his spirals, the image of the winding wire binding staying with me as I drive.

Two hours or so later I'm back; the house is empty, his car not in the garage. He's probably gone to Costco to buy the quinoa salad he likes. I can't know when he'll be back, but I go into his study anyway and look in his closet for the spirals. When he returns, I'll hear the garage door going up at the rear of the house and I can put a notebook back in the stack and get out before he comes in. But I can't find them. They're not on the shelf where he usually stores them, and I don't see them anywhere else. He has two storage tubs of old papers, and I pop the lid off the top one; no spirals, and same thing for the one on the bottom. I try his desk but don't see them in any of the drawers. Then I hear the door rolling up in the garage and shut all the drawers and make sure everything's in place. I go to the door and greet him.

It troubles me that I've snooped in his study. Why not just talk to him, say I'd like to know if what he's reading in them is weighing heavily on his mind, affecting him in a way I should know about? As I searched for the notebooks, I feared finding them. Am I prepared to read what's in their pages, to understand why he may have turned against his own story? Also troubling is the thought that he could have destroyed the notebooks or thrown them away. Did he take them somewhere in his car and drop them in a dumpster? What would that imply about how he sees his life? I give it thought and decide what I'll say to him.

He's in his study, seated at his desk, nothing in front of him. He stares ahead, looking stripped, abandoned. Or has he abandoned himself?

No notebook? I ask.

He pauses, choosing words to fill the gap without raising more questions. I could be wrong, but I don't think so.

Not today, he says.

Something's changing with you, and I think it has to do with your notebooks. Do you want me to leave you alone? I can do that.

I threw them out. I can't continue to delude myself that I was headed somewhere with the notebooks. I read through them all and at the end I couldn't look at them. Still, they're running through my head. I can't get away from them so easily. I don't know what else to say, but I can tell you that much.

Did you hope they'd be more than a record of your memories and experiences?

I can tell he doesn't want to answer, uncomfortable that he's exposed as much to me as he has. He's conflicted, not wanting to put me off or to let me in. Should he keep his mouth shut instead of satisfying my curiosity? What next then? Can either of us forget what we're talking about now? Does he intend to sit at his empty desk and stare into the void left by his notebooks? Maybe he needs time to grieve for them.

You've always been patient with me, he says. More so than I deserve.

Where are they? Can I get them back?

They're in the recycle bin in the driveway. But leave them there.

I'd like to read them. Are they embarrassing? I don't want to embarrass you.

They're worse. It's mainly because of everything that is not there. I would hate for you to see me that way. I should have burned them when you went out to lunch.

If you don't want me to read them, I won't. But in your mind they're still with you. I'll get them out of the bin and we can burn them together and you can mourn them.

I can't do it. I can't destroy them.

Should I bring them back in?

Not in here.

Can I save them?

Do what you want. Just don't tell me.

While he's taking a nap, I go out the door to the backyard

and unlock the gate, two big tote bags in hand. I'm afraid he'll wake up if I run the garage door up and down. I tip the recycling bin on its side, fish out his notebooks and stuff them in the totes. I hide them in the corner of a closet.

The next couple of days he rereads a novel by Kafka for maybe the tenth time since we've been married.

Three days after I retrieved the notebooks, late afternoon, I hear him snoozing in his study. He's muttering something, probably dreaming, but who knows where the words come from? I move close enough to hear him better. It sounds like *course* or *source* or *curse*, and he repeats the word or words.

His manner's changed during dinner, his gaze thawing, signs of life beneath his eyes.

In the morning, before we get out of bed, he asks me, Do you have them?

I'm reluctant to answer. The recycling truck passed yesterday. Has he been waiting for it?

Yes, I pulled them out.

Did you read them?

No.

You knew I'd regret not having them, didn't you?

I didn't, but I knew that if you changed your mind after they were gone you couldn't get them back.

I can't erase or deny what they say with some symbolic gesture. I need to see them and remember them, the wrong turns and disconnections. Wherever they've been, so have I.

When he goes to his study after breakfast, I bring the totes to him. He removes the notebooks and puts them on their shelf in his closet. Then he sits at his desk and pulls a new spiral notebook from a drawer. He seems at ease opening it to the first page and reaching for his pen as I watch.

I've surrendered to myself, he says. I'm starting again.

BOLGER

Bolger was not a friend of mine, but we had known each other for over twenty years, starting when he was married to his first wife and I was married to my only wife. I drank with him every couple of months at his café/bar, and it was there that he regularly held forth in a loud voice, repeating his favorite stories about himself to his audience of customers—how his shirt had caught fire in his café's kitchen, causing him to rip it off with his bare hands; how hot grease had spilled on his legs and burned through his trousers and he'd collapsed in a chair where his spirit had left his body, walked to a doorway and turned to see his sizzling flesh; how when skydiving his parachute had tangled in the static line and his reserve chute failed to open, forcing him to unpack it with his hands and toss it up in the air but too late to keep from crashing to the ground, where he claimed he'd bounced ten feet in the air.

I always sat with Bolger at his designated table just inside the front door of the bar, a place of honor reserved for those closest to him. For years he'd been trying to convince me to write his biography, though I'd never written for publication but only in a journal that I confessed to him I'd be ashamed for anyone to read. Bolger said he'd dictate the book to me, and he trusted me to portray him the way he wanted to be remembered. He enjoyed what he referred to as his fame in town, but he feared that after his death he'd gradually be forgotten. Bolger said that if I presented him in a disparaging way I knew he'd beat the hell out of me and he knew I'd fear that result. He roared with laughter and squeezed my head in the crook of his elbow. *Son*, he howled, though we were almost the same age and though he knew I didn't like him using his nickname for me. There were other things I didn't like about Bolger, including his loudness, drunkenness, womanizing, and megalomania. I seldom mentioned to him any of the sources of my distaste, and I only rarely took the floor when I was with him. When I did speak he didn't hesitate to interrupt me to greet people and hug them, and I'd hear his voice booming above the background music and ambient bar noise, his laughter cascading over the merriment of everyone around him. He'd come back to the table and fill me in on the people he'd spoken with, showing no memory of whatever I'd been saying to him. Bolger was consistently rude to his staff and he thought they respected him for his dominance, even those who outwardly resented it. He would snap his fingers at a passing server or hostess and order both of us another drink. If someone brought a drink with ice in it to the table, he would send the drink away. How long will it take you to remember this, he'd scold, no ice in any drinks at my table. He didn't like ice melting in his glass, and the space it occupied in a drink irked him. The servers often gave him a hostile look when he spoke to them curtly or snapped his fingers at them, but he didn't let himself be fazed. He would meet their look with one of his own, if he cared enough at a given moment to be bothered. Bolger had told me several stories of workers who'd tried to steal from him, which tended to happen more frequently near holidays. According to Bolger he'd confronted men with hams and quantities of beef concealed under their coats and he'd had fistfights with two of them in front of staff. He needed to make an example of them, he said, and confrontations and fighting were in some cases what was called for. He'd won both fights and had never failed to make a worker back down in conflicts that did not escalate to blows. Bolger told me he controlled everything about his environment. He wanted to be inside the head of everyone who worked for him, wanted them to hear his voice and to feel his grip. They had to feel him inside and outside or all hell would break loose, Bolger believed; he needed total control of everything around him to feel comfortable. He argued that the total-control principle would apply to his biography, a book that would serve as a monument to his life and that he envisaged with the title *Bolger*, with the letters in italics, he fittingly said, since he seemed to picture himself living his life in italics. Only he could know how the book should be written, only he could know what should be in the book and what should be left out. Bolger did not want to read and did not want others to read details about his sex life, he often said at his designated table; he wouldn't expose the dozens of married women he'd bedded, for example, and besides it would be bad for business and he'd rather not deal with a siege of threats. He knew I'd respect his reasons for withholding a thorough account of this side of him, Bolger said. His main concern about me as a biographer, he told me, though I'd consistently shown no interest in writing the book, was that I'd feel lingering loyalty toward his first wife and hold the circumstances surrounding the end of their fifteen-year marriage against him. He admitted he'd made a mistake on that one, without specifying what he wished he'd done differently, but he still failed to see why she couldn't accept the one affair she'd found out about when there had been over a hundred others she hadn't known about till he'd told her, Bolger declared with an utterly straight face. He'd tried to explain, he said, that being with other women was an essential part of his nature and she shouldn't be angered by it, but she couldn't embrace what he saw as the fully realized Bolger. His second wife couldn't accept this part of his nature either, and his third wife responded with aggression whenever she learned he'd been with another woman. For a long time he refused to divorce his third wife, because he knew that if he did he'd end up married again and divorced again. He contended that he cared less about his wives' anger over other women than about whether they would skin him alive, as he put it, in a divorce, not to mention, he added, what his own lawyers would see fit to charge him for their services. He couldn't take having his skin ripped off again, he said, even though his third wife liked to express her rage by assaulting him in his sleep. Bolger walked into the bar one day with two black eyes and a swollen nose after she had smashed a five-pound bag of ice on his face while he was taking a nap. I saw the black eyes myself and I asked him what had inspired the attack. I was bad, he confessed, and I thought he seemed somewhat proud of his injuries. He said that on another occasion she'd slugged him with her purse while he slept and another time with her fist. Bolger held firm on sticking with his third wife until he changed his mind one night when he awoke with a knife at his throat. His wives couldn't trust him to be at the bar with women hanging all over him there, said Bolger, as if the truth of his appeal to legions of women was self-evident. He and I were both in our mid-sixties and he'd confided that he supplemented his virility with a prescription drug. He said he didn't need the drug to perform but that it made him feel more powerful. Bolger informed me more than once that he'd bedded over a thousand women and I didn't ask how he counted them, if he wrote their names on a legal pad or if he entered them on some computer software or if he knew the names of all of them by heart along with locations of moles and birthmarks. I didn't ask him to estimate the number who were customers or if he ruled out wives of men he traded stories with, but occasionally a woman came into the bar that I could tell he'd been intimate with. He'd been with a long list of female staff, he told me, sometimes in his office with the door locked. Did he want other staff to know he was in his office screwing a young woman? I wondered but didn't ask. I steered clear of questions that would cause him to add details or embellish his narratives, sexual or otherwise. He never tired of the sound of his own voice, and he saw me as a person who didn't speak up enough. People wouldn't respect me as much as they should unless I spoke up more, he said. Verbally swaggering, Bolger told me he said and did whatever came to him at all times and he didn't care what anyone thought or how they reacted, and almost everyone respected him for speaking his mind and having things his way. On a trip the four of us took to Mexico, I'd been in the front seat of our rental car with Bolger driving while his first wife sat in back with my wife, the two of them talking nonstop and barely paying attention to us in front, their friendship the catalyst for our time together as couples. It annoyed him that I said I preferred not to drive in Mexico, a sign of cravenness unworthy of my gender as he saw it, and when I said as we rolled slowly through a town square that I wouldn't eat street food in Mexico, he pulled the car over and went to a stand to buy a hamburger and had the vendor cut it in two. He rushed back to the car and handed me half. Eat it, he said. I shook my head. Eat it, he repeated and bit into the burger. It's good. Eat it! he said again. Isn't it good? he asked as I took my first taste. *Son,* he shouted, jabbing me. Just as he'd forced the hamburger on me in Mexico, Bolger kept pushing drinks at me in his bar, though I left some of them untouched on the table, even pouring two or three into a nearby plant just to get rid of them. I couldn't imagine how his body could have endured all the drinks he'd consumed in his life. The skin on his face had become increasingly dark, particularly around his eyes, his mustache increasingly gray, and his back had begun to curve in a way that suggested a question mark and subdued his strut. How many more drinks could he absorb, his body seemed to be asking him, but his voice still boomed out of him and his belief in his importance remained unchanged. I thought of the mass of people as *the sales force*, I'd told Bolger on a night when I'd had more to drink than normal, the people in the sales force seeing it as their mission to sell an idea or self-image or a version of their past, the effort extending to the deepest parts of their own awareness and existence. He saw people as customers, I said to him, and in my opinion that represented our fundamental difference. The truth is we're all members of the sales force, he answered, but we're also customers. You can't separate these things in people. In your case, you don't want to see yourself as being in the sales force or as a customer, he lamented, and I don't think you even like to hear yourself talk. You'd rather listen to me, although I doubt if you agree with a thing I'm saying. I saw at once that my view of people as members of the sales force would stay with Bolger and that he would see it as symptomatic of my deficiencies as a man, just as he saw my aversion to eating street food in Mexico as symptomatic of a squeamishness that would keep me from growing into the actualized man he'd become. How could I hope to control my environment, I thought he thought, unless I accepted being in the sales force? Those who did accept their sales-force position would surpass me without noticing that I existed; how could I make any sort of impression on anyone or anything unless I made an effort to enhance my status in the sales force? I disliked what I saw when I saw myself through his eyes, and I invariably felt relieved to push away from his table, taking the opportunity to flee when he greeted an incoming couple or group. I always left his bar fed up with him, talking back to the memory of his face. What did I have to do with Bolger and why did I listen to him? I pondered a reasonable explanation for my visits, and he must have too. He sometimes asked me if I had something to confess to him, and he'd stare at me as if his eyes could pry out the words he thought might be forthcoming. Whenever he asked me this question, I denied having a confession to make, but he appeared unsure whether to believe me. I finally asked him what was on his mind about what he thought I had on my mind. I'd come into the bar late and Bolger's face had begun to sag, but the weight of the day's drinks did not interfere with his power of speech. He asked if I ever had any inkling that his first wife had been interested in me and had used me as an example of how he might behave better if he ever chose to improve himself. She liked being around a quiet man, she'd said, though she had to know when she married Bolger that she was forming a union with a loudmouth. Though Bolger believed he was entitled to have sex with any number of other women, what he admitted to me was his suspicion that I'd slept with his first wife, not while he was married to her, I didn't have the guts to do that, he commented, but sometime after their divorce and probably after mine. He fantasized that she may have been the one to initiate contact, but he wanted to hear the true story from me, man to man. I replied that I hadn't slept with any of his wives or ex-wives or any other woman he'd slept with, as far as I knew, and his first wife had said nothing to suggest she was ever attracted to me. You don't have to worry about what I'll do if you admit it, Bolger said, what she does is up to her. I don't follow her or ask around about her business, but you come in here and look me in the eye and drink with me and I want to know who I'm drinking with, who's listening to me and what's underneath the way you listen. The bottom line is that you think I'm some kind of animal, don't you, you think I'm like some wild dog or a bull trampling through everything that gets in my way. I think the reason you don't want to write my biography is that you don't have the nerve to write what you want to write and you won't write what I want you to write. You couldn't face a book that you wrote about me being sold in this bar and to be responsible for whichever version would be in its pages. Maybe it was a bad idea asking you to write the book, your outlook is too limited to see my life the way I do. Do you think I don't know what you see when you look at me? Do you want to hear why I think you come here? Either you want to confess that you slept with H— or you want to listen to me long enough to convince yourself over and over that you can't stand the sound of people talking, especially not me, and you get so disgusted by what comes out of my mouth that you can last maybe two months in virtual seclusion, limiting contact to trips out for food and passersby who don't really see you personally. You can't avoid speaking to people from time to time, but you're not at ease speaking or listening to them and you look forward to your stretches of silence. You sit with your journal, waiting for something meaningful to show its face, until you get bored and creep out of your hole to be around people again, and then you come to me for your people-revulsion fix. Does any of that sound familiar? Bolger asked, his characterization of me based on conjecture and snippets of comments I'd made to him in years past. Had he told me off to trigger a confession about sleeping with H— or to browbeat me into admitting why I wouldn't write his biography? He waited, expecting me to speak, giving the impression that his eyes would not release me. But I had nothing to tell him about sleeping with his first wife and nothing to reveal about fearing which version I'd choose to write in an imaginary book about him. I resented that he wanted to push me into a corner, to dominate me through provocation, but I didn't want to leave without answering him. I'd listened to his thunder for twenty-plus years and I'd never had a serious confrontation with him. Why not? What did I fear would happen? I told Bolger that in my opinion he wasn't biography material, almost no one would read a book about him, and if anyone did his enemies might be as likely to read it as his admirers. The release of a biography might cause social media to light up with stories from people he'd intimidated with violence or threats and he'd probably seem more outrageous to others than he'd ever imagined. I felt no desire at all to write a book about him and no desire to be with any woman he'd ever been with. I thought the most important thing he did not understand about his first wife was that she wanted to be loved in an uncompromised way, just as he did. I then confessed that I did not like the sound of my voice or his and that I was exhausted when I left his company. I did retreat into a period of relative solitude, I said, waiting for the noise of his voice and the inevitable repetition of its content to subside in my memory, though in time the silence became tedious and the urge to hear other voices returned. The best reason I had come up with for why I listened to Bolger was that I wanted to understand him, to believe he wanted something more than control of everyone and everything within his reach. I wanted to see something redeeming in his relentless need for conquest, but I hadn't found it, I said straight into his more or less expressionless face, and I could only listen to him for so long before his voice overwhelmed my curiosity. The food in his café was widely known to be terrible, but his drinks were known to be tasty, and I appreciated his apparent hospitality, though I suspected that, like anything else he did, it contained a self-serving motive, perhaps to have a book written about him or to learn information about H—'s sex life or a deep-seated need to sell his image of himself. Bolger didn't flinch once as I spoke and when I finished he chuckled. *Son,* he bellowed and squeezed my shoulder with his non-drink hand. I think I'll speak with some other members of the sales force, he said, and he stood and joined acquaintances at the bar as if nothing had happened. I stayed a little while, not wanting to leave too quickly, to act out my fear that he'd decide to retaliate. As soon as I did leave, listening for footsteps behind me but hearing none, I began to wonder if I would ever go back and, if I did, how he would react when he saw me and if we would sit at his table and have a drink.

I went three months without entering Bolger's bar, but I heard his voice immediately when I returned, his chute tangled in the static line once again, his body bouncing off the ground, landing him in a hospital bed for weeks. I sat at his table and ordered a drink, and after a few minutes he noticed me there and came over. He shook my hand but did not sit down. I called her, he told me. She said you had nothing to confess. She was furious that I asked her, and if she ever speaks to me again it won't be because she started the conversation. She asked what it had to do with me. I told her that if you did have something to confess, I'd ask you that question. But bottom line, I know she wouldn't lie to me. He smiled as he watched his words sink in. I've spent countless hours drinking in that chair, he said. Are you sure you want to sit in it? He gave me a look before leaving me alone at the table, and I sat there considering why he would believe her and not me and why he would intrude on her with his question. Would he have seen my sleeping with her as a challenge to his superiority, a convoluted threat, an expression of an undermining desire that may have been there for almost as long as we'd known one another? And why did he care now? Answers to my questions were beyond my reach and perhaps beyond his. Bolger circulated at the bar, his voice and laughter filling the air around him, his romance with himself undiminished.

One month later, he died from a stroke.

Acknowledgments:

"Buffalo" *The Literarian*
"Faux Bois" *The Rupture*
"Tunnel" *The Los Angeles Review*
"Contact" *Hobart* (Web)
"Connect" *New Ohio Review*
"Host" *Green Mountains Review* Online
"Due" *The Rupture*
"Shepherd" *The Rupture*
"Self-Service" *failbetter*
"Table" *New World Writing*
"Sync" *The Rupture*
"Dinner" *Cimarron Review*
"Getaway" *Little Star*
"From" *The Saint Ann's Review*
"Shirl" *Gravel*
"Hotel Room" *The Antioch Review*
"Intruder" *Green Mountains Review* Online
"Surrender" *AGNI* Online
"Bolger" *Green Mountains Review* Online

For Linda,
my heart and soul,
with love

Glen Pourciau's first story collection won the 2008 Iowa Short Fiction Award. His short story, "Gone," won the 2004 Carter V. Cooper Memorial Prize in Short Fiction, published by *Ontario Review*. His short story, "Deep Wilderness," won the Texas Institute of Letters short story award. His most recent collection, *View*, was published by Four Way Books in 2017. He lives in Galveston, TX.

Publication of this book was made possible by grants and donations. We are also grateful to those individuals who participated in our 2020 Build a Book Program. They are:

Anonymous (14), Robert Abrams, Nancy Allen, Maggie Anderson, Sally Ball, Matt Bell, Laurel Blossom, Adam Bohannon, Lee Briccetti, Therese Broderick, Jane Martha Brox, Christopher Bursk, Liam Callanan, Anthony Cappo, Carla & Steven Carlson, Paul & Brandy Carlson, Renee Carlson, Cyrus Cassells, Robin Rosen Chang, Jaye Chen, Edward W. Clark, Andrea Cohen, Ellen Cosgrove, Peter Coyote, Janet S. Crossen, Kim & David Daniels, Brian Komei Dempster, Matthew DeNichilo, Carl Dennis, Patrick Donnelly, Charles Douthat, Morgan Driscoll, Lynn Emanuel, Monica Ferrell, Elliot Figman, Laura Fjeld, Michael Foran, Jennifer Franklin, Sarah Freligh, Helen Fremont & Donna Thagard, Reginald Gibbons, Jean & Jay Glassman, Ginny Gordon, Lauri Grossman, Naomi Guttman & Jonathan Mead, Mark Halliday, Beth Harrison, Jeffrey Harrison, Page Hill Starzinger, Deming Holleran, Joan Houlihan, Thomas & Autumn Howard, Elizabeth Jackson, Christopher Johanson, Voki Kalfayan, Maeve Kinkead, David Lee, Jen Levitt, Howard Levy, Owen Lewis, Jennifer Litt, Sara London & Dean Albarelli, David Long, James Longenbach, Excelsior Love, Ralph & Mary Ann Lowen, Jacquelyn Malone, Donna Masini, Catherine McArthur, Nathan McClain, Richard McCormick, Victoria McCoy, Ellen McCulloch-Lovell, Judith McGrath, Debbie & Steve Modzelewski, Rajiv Mohabir, James T. F. Moore, Beth Morris, John Murillo & Nicole Sealey, Michael & Nancy Murphy, Maria Nazos, Kimberly Nunes, Bill O'Brien, Susan Okie & Walter Weiss, Rebecca Okrent, Sam Perkins, Megan Pinto, Kyle Potvin, Glen Pourciau, Kevin Prufer, Barbara Ras, Victoria Redel, Martha Rhodes, Paula Rhodes, Paula Ristuccia, George & Nancy Rosenfeld, M. L. Samios, Peter & Jill Schireson, Rob Schlegel, Roni & Richard Schotter, Jane Scovell, Andrew Seligsohn & Martina Anderson, James & Nancy Shalek, Soraya Shalforoosh, Peggy Shinner, Dara-Lyn Shrager, Joan Silber, Emily Sinclair, James Snyder & Krista Fragos, Alice St. Claire-Long, Megan Staffel, Bonnie Stetson, Yerra Sugarman, Dorothy Tapper Goldman, Marjorie & Lew Tesser, Earl Teteak, Parker & Phyllis Towle, Pauline Uchmanowicz, Rosalynde Vas Dias, Connie Voisine, Valerie Wallace, Doris Warriner, Ellen Doré Watson, Martha Webster & Robert Fuentes, Calvin Wei, Bill Wenthe, Allison Benis White, Michelle Whittaker, and Ira Zapin.